*Love, Patience and Time*

Primix Publishing
11620 Wilshire Blvd
Suite 900, West Wilshire Center, Los Angeles, CA, 90025
www.primixpublishing.com
Phone: 1-800-538-5788



Published by Primix Publishing: 05/22/2024

ISBN: 979-8-89194-046-8(sc)
ISBN: 979-8-89194-047-5(e)

Library of Congress Control Number: 2024900917

# Forward

*I have compiled several short stories of love based on fantasy, eliminating all the typical day-to-day drama that we face and is often written about. What I would like to give my readers is an opportunity to see love through a different view, one, in my opinion, that we have forgotten can exist. I invite you to enter a world of love and true appreciation; let your mind go and feel the love and passion that is expressed in each story.*

*Enjoy...*

# Acknowledgments

Special thanks to my husband Antwan and my daughter Ontaria for their love, patience and understanding.

Thanks to all those who turned me away, let me go and closed me out because it opened new possibilities to grow!  Woot!  Woot!

# Table of Contents

*"I believe in the power inside of my heart...God is the source from whom we're never apart...No challenge to great and no cause is too small...this infinite love is inside of us all,"*

*Eric Benet...Love, Patience and Time from the Love and Life CD*

# Cafe

I don't know where the saying "art imitates life" originated, but it is really true; Alicia Keys' song, *You Don't Know My Name* is written about me. When I saw the music video, I almost fell out my chair; it's almost like she was somewhere watching my life transpire, it's my favorite video.

I have been working at Bailey's Café for six months. It's my first time working as a waitress, it was tough at first, but I have gotten into the swing of things, and I am enjoying it.

Of course, my friends think I am crazy as hell, given my education and past work experiences. I have an MBA and have been in the Training industry for more than twenty years. I started as a facilitator, was an instructional designer and finished as the Director of Training. I have worked at several Fortune 500 and 100 companies which are impressive on the resume but never lasted long as a result of multiple layoffs. For whatever reason, I am always in the number to be let go. No matter how hard I worked, how flexible, how much of a team player and accommodating I was, the axe always had my name on it. After this last layoff I could not stomach another job interview, another promise of success and great benefits; I have decided to become my own boss and open a career development center for adults re-entering the workforce.

I realized early in life that I had a gift for mentoring and educating others. If any of my friends or family needed advice or encouragement, I was usually the person that was sought out. My mother suggested counseling or becoming a schoolteacher but neither of those interested me. My major in college was marketing because I had a strong interest in advertising, but after attending a time management workshop during a summer internship, I knew being a facilitator was my calling. I began to research careers in training and the rest is history. Once Prime Cable laid me off, I decided that my next step would be to follow my dreams. While I put my plan into motion, I am working here at Bailey's.

Bailey Jefferson owns several restaurants in the area. I always ate at his larger, more upscale French-themed restaurant, C'est Bon on the North side of town. They serve a great spinach and sun-dried tomato pasta; light and filling at the same time. They also have an amazing veal parmesan, and the buttered rolls almost melt in your mouth. I would go there about twice a month and eventually became a noticeable regular, often getting preference on seating and occasionally a complimentary dessert.

I have learned that you should always treat people with respect no matter what their role is in life; I have benefited as a result. I cannot tell you how many times I have been given free admission to events, parked where I wasn't supposed to and a number of freebies just because of my pleasant personality. We all work together, and we are all each other's customers; why should I look down on a person who is serving my food, opening a door, or cleaning up my mess when they are doing something for me? I eat out because I do not want to cook on that day; so, it is a service for me to go out and eat and then go home and put my feet up. I appreciate having someone else cook the food and serve it to me. In return I am helping them stay employed by coming to the restaurant, paying for my food, and tipping; it all works together. So, I always smile and converse with any and everybody I encounter daily; it is a practice that has paid off.

One night my girls and I were having one of our monthly outings at C'est Bon and Bailey came over and introduced himself, he commented on the frequency of my visits and thanked me for my patronage. He gave me my meal free and bought drinks for my girls. He left his card and told me to call him if I was ever in need of anything. I never called, but for the next year every time I came in, we always held small conversations. I found out he was married with three kids and five grandchildren. He had been in the restaurant business for over forty years. He was a very nice man and as it turned out, a good person to know.

The day I was laid off, I went to C'est Bon and, instead of getting a table; I went straight to the bar with the idea of getting smashed and calling an Uber or Lyft to take me home. Surprised to see me sitting at the bar, Bailey came over with a look of true concern in his eyes that was very touching. I told him what happened and expressed my frustration with life in Corporate America. I shared that I felt like a mouse spinning around in that little wheel going nowhere.

"I truly know how you feel," Bailey said, "C'est Bon was started from some of the same frustration." I didn't experience layoffs; I just grew tired helping someone else be successful and not being appreciated."

"Yes, not being appreciated is even more frustrating than being laid off," I said as I took another sip of my drink.

Bailey gave me a look of concern and placed his hand on my back, "I have an opening if you are interested."

I nearly choked on my drink; I felt appalled that he would offer me a job as a waitress and then I immediately felt a little hypocritical. While I truly am acceptable of everyone, I could not see myself working as a waitress.

"I have never worked as a server, I replied trying not to offend him, "I do not know that I am cut out to carry trays and get orders correct. I have watched your servers, and it doesn't look like an easy job."

"Being a server is more about personality than carrying server trays and getting orders correct. We have an excellent training program, and you have a wonderful personality so I am sure you will do just fine," Bailey said.

"I am not so sure Bailey," I replied.

I didn't know how to tell him that this position would not fit in my social circle, I couldn't even imagine telling my girls that I had accepted a job as a waitress.

"My staff made close to $25,000 last year in just tips," Bailey said as though he could read my mind, "This put them at an annual salary of $33,000."

I almost laughed in his face at first; given this is a third of the salary that I made at Prime Cable.

"Bailey, I can't tell you how much your offer means to me, you are a wonderful man," I said as smiled appreciatively.

Bailey smiled at me and stood to leave me sulking at the bar. "I will give you a little time to think about it I am not in a big hurry to fill the position and the drinks are on me tonight."

"Thanks Bailey," I said as my eyes filled with tears.

"You are truly welcome, your presence in my restaurant is always welcomed, you are appreciated. Please think about my offer, it may not be the salary that you are accustomed to, but it will be something while you get your thoughts and plans together."

With that he placed a kiss on my forehead and walked away.

The next morning as I opened my eyes to the sun rays streaming through my wood blinds, I heard Bailey's last words to me from the night before, *it may not be the salary that you are accustomed to but it will be something while you get your thoughts and plans together* and it became clear that this would be a good break for me while I planned my next move. I have managed my money well throughout my career, so making less would not put me in a financial bind. With what I have saved and my one-year severance, this salary would keep me from falling into depression mode and give me time to plan for my Career Development Center. I rolled over and grabbed my cell phone to call Bailey.

"Good morning, Bailey George," he said as he cleared his throat.

"Good morning, Bailey, the first thing I heard when I awoke this morning was your voice so I have decided to accept your offer," I said with excitement.

"I am glad to hear that Kimberly, I promise you won't regret it," he said pleased with my decision. "Let's see," he began as I heard paper rattling on his desk. "If you can come in first thing Monday morning and complete your paperwork, you can start training on that afternoon."

"That's great Bailey, I really appreciate you!" I said with excitement and a little bit of nervousness.

I didn't know at the time that the job would not be at C'est Bon, but at his Cafe. It was a shock when I showed up on Monday to complete my paperwork and was given directions to the Café to complete my training. I immediately began to second-guess my decision, and quickly placed a call to Bailey, but he promised me that the earning potential would be just as great at his Café. I began work the following week and have enjoyed it.

I had been at the Café for a month before I noticed a regular customer that came in every Tuesday at 1:30 p.m. like clockwork. No matter what he ordered, he always had a cup of green tea with mint. His order of the green tea caught my attention because it was my idea to add herbal teas to the menu and he was proof that the idea worked; I was flattered.

He always sat on my co-worker, Sheila's side of the counter, so I never had a chance to serve him. I would glance at him occasionally, but I have never made eye contact because his head was always buried deep into whatever he was reading.

This is where the Alicia Keys video kicks in because just like Mos Def in the video, he barely, if ever, looks at me; he orders his food and buries his head in a newspaper or book.

I really liked that he was a reader because I love to read myself. He typically reads the classic intellectuals like W.E.B. DuBois, or Langston Hughes; levels I haven't reached yet, although I do have one of Langston Hughes's books of poetry.

It is rare to see an African American man reading leisurely so when I see one, I typically ask what they are reading. However, I never said anything to him because, while he was never rude to me, he appeared somewhat standoffish, and I didn't want my inquiring about his reading to look like I was flirting.

That is the difference between my situation and Alicia Keys. I don't care how fine and attractive this brother is…and he is; if you don't have a welcoming demeanor, I keep my distance.

I had been at Bailey's for four months and going through the same routine every Tuesday at 1:30 p.m. with my mystery man; however, this would not be a routine. The mystery man had come in like normal, ordering the regular. He had been there for about 30 minutes before I even paid attention to him. When things freed up for me and I had a chance to glance over, I noticed he was reading my favorite book *In Search of Satisfaction* by one of the world's greatest and most prolific authors J. California Cooper. Before I knew it, I was standing in front of him full of excitement. "I absolutely love that woman's work!" I couldn't help myself, I had to say something and looking back, I am truly glad I did…

******************

Thank God it's Tuesday, time for me to slip off to my secret spot and enjoy a little quiet time with the folk on the other side of town. This was the best idea I could have ever had for myself. I can tolerate the Corporate America bullshit a whole lot better when I can slip away and be with some real people.

Eating with people who you don't care for, and you know don't really like you can cause some serious heartburn issues. I really enjoy the work that I do and have worked hard to acquire the things that bring me joy. I have been blessed to own my dream car, a 650i Vermillion Red BMW, the car of the Kappa Man that I am. I have a nice condo on in the district, the area for the up-and-coming business executives. The district is a six-block community of residential properties, retail business and restaurants. A Starbucks is in the center of the six blocks and resembles a water hole where everyone gathers to mix and mingle. Living in the district is something that is sought out by many but only achieved by a few. People are not known to move frequently so when a place becomes available you must jump on it; I am fortunate to have purchased my condo during the development phase. I now have a nice amount of equity since the value has nearly doubled.

I also take two vacations a year; my friends call me the travel advisor. I visit one new place a year; alternating each year between a place in the United States and overseas and I take three or four days at my timeshare on Myrtle Beach. I know I could not afford these things if it were not for my job so I deal with the fallacies the best way I can…which includes my weekly escape.

I have learned that the best way to be successful and stay that way is to encircle yourself with those people who think like you and share the same goals. Unfortunately, those people are typically very fake and are not who you would call loyal friends. In the circles I travel in, you have more associates than friends, we have great discussions and an occasional enjoyable time, but I don't typically share any intimate details. I am fortunate to have one faithful friend in my circle, Bernard, he and I met in college and have climbed our corporate ladders of success together, never missing a beat in our friendship. I thank God for him every day. But, even in our bond, he suffers from the upper-lower class mentality which causes the need to break from him sometimes as well, hence my Tuesday afternoon escapes.

I found this restaurant looking through the food section in the newspaper. I like to cook and every Thursday, the local paper has a food section with great recipes and reviews of restaurants. Bailey's Café was listed as a great Soul Food restaurant. It really seemed like a cool place from the pictures, and it received great reviews; but like a lot of restaurants with this theme, it was not on the ideal side of town. I was hooked on my first visit and have been a faithful customer ever since. The wait staff is really great, and because I tip well, I can tell that I am a favorite.

I had been going for a year and was familiar with all of the waitresses; none of which ever caught my eye for one reason or another. One Tuesday I came in expecting to see the same faces but was greeted by a new waitress that nearly took my breath away. She was 5 feet 10 inches of fineness that would make a blind man see. She had smooth chocolate skin tone that reminded me of chocolate in a Milky Way bar. And when she turned around and I saw that God had truly favored her with a treasure that most black men love, I almost lost my mind. Everybody knows that black men love ass, and I am not an exception to the rule.

I judge women by the size of the ass, if they don't have one, they don't have me…plain and simple; and this is one that I would love to have, if she worked on my side of town.

How could I explain her to my boy Bernie, *yeah man I'm dating this waitress at the café that I sneak off to every Tuesday*, I can't do it.

I considered forming a relationship with her and keeping it a secret. We could go to the movies on this side of town, I wouldn't run into anyone I know and wouldn't have to explain. Then I realized that I'm too old for that shit; if I spend time with someone, I want it to be full-time, go anywhere do anything basis. I don't have the energy for the lying and manipulating games anymore, this will just have to be one ass that I pass up.

To keep myself from even thinking of starting anything with this fine specimen, I made sure that I brought in something to read, which helped me keep up with my reading. I have always loved to read and have gotten heavy into Tavis Smiley. The love of reading was developed by my aunt who owned a bookstore. I would work there during the summer. She would always threaten to fire me because I would always get caught reading in a corner rather than working; but she never did because she knew reading kept me out of the trouble that so many boys my age were getting into.

At one of my visits to the bookstore, I finally picked up a book, *Piece of Mind*, by my aunt's favorite author J. California Cooper. When I was younger, Ms. Cooper had held several book signings at my aunt's bookstore, but she had never interested me; now that I have matured, I enjoy her storytelling and ability to incorporate life lessons in her stories. The book is a great collection of short stories dealing with the everyday trials of life and relationships. I have to agree with my aunt when she says that Cooper teaches you about life and how to deal with people.

After I finished her collection of short stories, *Piece of Mine*, I purchased one of her novels, *In Search of Satisfaction* which I was really enjoying.

Another Tuesday had rolled around so I took the book to the Café with the intent of getting deeper into the story line and keeping my mind and eyes off Milky Way.

I was a little disappointed when I didn't see her, but I figured she must have had a day off, so I placed my order, a veggie burger with cheese on a wheat bun, sweet potato fries and mint green tea with Sheila, my regular waitress and began to read my book.

As my tea was being placed in front of me, I heard an excited voice say, "That is one of my most favorite books!"  What part are you on?"

I looked up and it was the Milky Way. Part of my avoidance of her was not really looking at her so I never noticed that she had a beautiful smile and pretty brown eyes that seemed to be a mirror to her soul. Shocked that she had finally said something to me I couldn't respond right away, so I just stared blankly, which she mistook as a rude jester of me saying that I didn't want to talk.

The twinkle in her eye and smile quickly turned to an embarrassed *excuse me I didn't mean to disturb you, nigger please* kind of a look and she turned to walk away. I immediately reached out and grabbed her hand and explained that she had caught me off guard. I introduced myself and answered her question. She said her name was Kimberly Stewart; a perfect name to match the warm smile she gave me at first. We talked briefly about the book and other books that were our favorites then she walked away.  The conversation was cordial, but I could tell that I had given the wrong impression.

Just as I was finishing my meal, I noticed she had her purse and was leaving. She was telling everyone goodbye for the day and was making her way out the door. I took the last bite of the burger, stuffed the remaining fries in my mouth, threw $20 on the counter and ran out the door to catch her.

She had made it about a block and a half from the café by the time I caught up with her, God she walks fast; but I managed to catch her just as she was walking into the Payless Shoe store; another confirmation that this would not work.

When I caught up with her, she looked a little embarrassed but I opened the door for her and we went in.

"Kimberly," I said slightly out of breath. "I am really sorry if I offended you back there."

"No worries, umm what did you say your name was again?" she said with a dry smile.

"It's Michael Lattimore" I said slightly annoyed because I knew she was being cynical.

"Yes, that's right. Michael, you didn't need to follow me here to say that" she said.

"I really apologize, I am so use to coming in, ordering my lunch and not holding a conversation; I was surprised to hear your voice and even more surprised at how beautiful your eyes and smile are."

She gave me a look like she thought I was full of shit and said, "I understand, you never talk to anyone, so I don't know why I thought you would be interested in having a conversation with me." She folded her hands across her chest, "It's really no big deal, you didn't have to follow me here to say that, I won't spit on your food or anything," she said sarcastically.

"I am not worried about that, I am a really nice guy, and I don't want you to get the wrong impression about me," I said with a slight smile.

"Well again, you don't have to worry and thanks for explaining yourself…no harm no foul," She said as she walked down the women's size 8-10 aisle.

I followed her down the aisle and continued with the small talk. She explained that she was picking up a pair of sandals to where to a cookout. She appeared uncomfortable with being in a discount shoe store, so she went on to explain that she buys her cute and fashionable shoes at Payless and the quality shoes that she wears every day at other stores. I wanted to say, *yeah right,* because I felt she was trying to put on airs for me. Here I was in a Giorgio Armani Suit and here she was in a waitress outfit shopping at Payless; I know she must have felt extremely out of her league. However, being the gentleman that I am, I pretended like I understood exactly where she was coming from. I must admit, the sandals that she bought were pretty fly and they looked awesome on her feet and complimented those gorgeous legs. I almost grabbed myself looking at the view.

After she made her purchase, we headed back in the direction of the Café.

"Your lunch break is over then?" I asked.

"No, I am finished for the day," she responded. "I am going to get a quick work out in before I head home."

"Oh yeah, where do you work out?" I asked, now understanding why the body was so fly.

"Over at the City Athletic Club downtown, I 've been working out there for three years now," she said, getting more comfortable with the conversation.

I couldn't believe what I was hearing. That is the most posh fitness club around. How could someone who works at a café on this side of town afford to work out and fit in with the crowd there? That is a gym where only the elite corporate executives and corporate up and comings work out.

Before I knew it, I was asking, "How did you get a membership there?"

I immediately knew I had offended her because she gave me that same look when she first asked me about the book.

"Excuse me, I didn't know that someone like me couldn't work out there, but if you must know I was Director of Training and Development at Prime Cable before their massive layoff. I still had some time left and my Vice President added three years to my membership as an appreciation gift," she said as she snatched her keys out of her purse and pressed the unlock button.

I knew from the tone and the slight twist in her neck that I had totally offended her and didn't know what to do about it. I truly didn't want to offend her, and I didn't want her to get the wrong impression about me. I have my ways, but I am genuinely a nice guy.

She abruptly turned and walked away. I hadn't noticed that we had made our way to the parking lot, so I ran up to her as she approached her car, a BMW 530i. It was a Deep Sea Blue color with beige interior. You could tell she maintained it well getting it regularly washed and waxed. I walked up to her and grabbed her hand as she was about to open her car door and begged her to give me another chance. I obviously had misjudged her and was feeling like a complete fool. Regardless of what Bernard or anyone else would think, this was someone I wanted to get to know better…a lot better.

"Look I am truly sorry, can I please make it up to you over dinner tonight," I asked in a desperate plea, "I have really enjoyed talking to you and I would love to get to know you better. I can even help find you a better job."

She looked at me and politely said, "Thank you, but who said that I wanted a *better* job?  And who said that this is not *the* job for me?"

"You are the reason why I am so tired of Corporate America and all if it's fakeness and perpetrators!" she said with a frown.

She paused and I knew that I had placed my foot in my mouth again. She looked at me, raised her finger and continued.

"You and the people like you are the reason I chose to work in the Café. I am so tired chasing all the carrots that are put out there for us to make us feel like we have achieved when we have not. The business cards, offices with nice furniture, titles, and stock options, all make us feel like we are climbing the ladder, when in all actuality we are not. I make less money working here, but I am happier and more at peace than I have ever been. So, thank you, but no thank you, I will pass,"

Not wanting to give up, I gave a quick response.

"Fine, then let me cook you dinner and we won't even talk about work or Corporate America, I just don't want to lose an opportunity of developing a great relationship with you…Please," I gave her my puppy dog look; the slight smile with my head tilted to the side and dropped my eyes a little.

This look always worked with my mom and her sisters, and it appeared to be working here because she gave me a slight smile and said okay. We set a date for tomorrow night, she handed me her number and left.

******************

We really got off to a shaky start. As I could tell from his Giorgio Armani suits and his general attitude when he came to the Café; he was the typical I got a good paying job with benefits and a nice title so you can't touch me brothers.

When he followed me down to Payless I could have screamed because I know he was thinking this was all I could afford, but he was wrong. There was no way in hell I was going to pay top dollar for shoes that will go out of style in a couple of years. I always bought my cute fashion, just kick it every now and then shoes from Payless and my quality work shoes from Dillards or Nordstrom's. But I wasn't going to get into all that with him. The expression on his face when I told him where I worked out really said it all. I enjoyed putting him in his place though; he really looked dumb when I told him where I worked prior to Bailey's.

He really had a nerve, offering to help me find a job, as if I couldn't find work if I wanted to; but I did love his persistence in offering to take me on a date. I may change my mind though; I don't want to give the wrong impression by going to his home and allowing him to cook for me.

My thinking has always been that going to a man's home is telling him that you will sleep with him. Although he is a fine specimen, I am not ready to make that move; well I am, but I have to make a good first impression.

I may give him a call later, damn, I didn't get his number, I only gave him mine. If he is sincere, he will call tonight, and I can let him know that I would rather go to C'est Bon for dinner.

I had just walked in from an excellent work out at the gym when the phone rang. I didn't recognize the number but was pleasantly surprised when I heard his voice on the other line.

"Hi, I am just calling to find out what kind of things you like to eat. I don't want to cook something that you wouldn't like," he said with a laugh.

I knew it, maybe he is sincere and a pretty nice guy.

"Well…," I replied hesitantly, "I was really thinking that it might be better if we meet up at C'est Bon. It is one of my favorite restaurants and I really enjoy the food there,"

"Oh, why can't I cook for you, are you scared you won't be able to control yourself if you are alone with me?" he asked jokingly.

"Oh please, I replied, if anything I would be afraid that you wouldn't be able to control yourself. I don't want to be on the six o'clock news going, *it was just a dinner date*. And have all the women saying, *you knew you were going to have to give him some if you went to his apartment.*"

We both laughed at that one and he became more serious and said, "I would not risk everything I've worked for, for something that I can get at a drop of a hat, and I like you enough to wait as long as I need to for that."

I don't know what it was about what he said but I felt a twinge of excitement from his tone and the fact that he would and had even thought of getting some of this.

"Well, I really like Italian, but I am starting to get into seafood a little more so anything along those lines would be great. I really do not have too many things that I don't like."

He let out a soft sexy chuckle and asked me what time I would like to have dinner and whether I would like for him to come get me or drive over to his place. I told him I would drive; I like to be in control, and that 7 p.m. would be great. We talked for a few moments, and I ended the conversation by saying that I needed to get a shower and run a couple of errands.

I ran to my closet to try to find something to wear and remembered a dress I saw at Nordstrom's that would really set my Payless sandals off. I wanted to wear the sandals so he could see how nice they really were and that if he didn't know they were from Payless they could look as good as any shoes bought from a higher priced store. I had two hours to shower and throw on something and headed to Nordstrom's.

God is good, not only was the dress still there, but it was 30% off. It was a sleeveless A-line dress falling just above my knee. The dress really had a tropical feel to it with a mixture of apricot, ocean blue and green. The pattern was soft enough not be considered loud. It fit like it was tailor made, accentuating all my curves. Three ladies complimented me in the dressing room, so it looks like it will be a winner.

Mission accomplished, I went home fixed a salad and tried to watch a little television to take my mind off tomorrow evening. I was thankful that I had to work tomorrow or else I would be stuck sitting home watching the time go by. I can't believe I was acting this way; it was at that time that I realized that I had not actually been on a date since I had begun working at the café. I have not dated anyone seriously since Rahman re-located three years ago.

I always had guys asking me out when I worked at Prime Cable, but I had an established a rule that I would never date anyone that I worked with. That was until I met Rahman a contractor in the IT department. I went against my own rules and justified it because he was a contractor with a six-month assignment. I figured it wouldn't hurt anything because his time with the company was limited. That turned out not to be true because his contract kept getting extended and six months turned into two years. I should have known things were not going to be good after our third date and a weekend of off the chain sex, he came to my desk the following Monday and said, "this weekend was good, tell me know who I need to beat up?" He tried to laugh it off, but I was a little offended and scared. Why did he assume there was someone else in the company I was sleeping with? Did he think I got around like that? Was he about to go fight someone if I was? When I said that to him, he immediately backed off and kept saying that he was joking. We had a great relationship, it never interfered with my job, and we kept it discreet so no one would know. His contract finally ended, and he accepted another assignment out of state. We talk occasionally, but not too often and never for an extended period of time. These last three years I have managed to keep myself pretty busy between the gym and blind dates, which there haven't been many of. So, in all actuality it had been a while, and I was really looking forward to tomorrow evening. I had an early shift tomorrow, so to keep my mind off my date with Michael, I went to bed early.

*********************

I kept going over the day's events not believing that I had a date with Milky Way; Kimberly is a nice name, but this will be my personal name for her. Even more amazing is the fact that I am cooking her dinner. Don't get me wrong, I have cooked my share of dinners for ladies, after all, it is in chapter nine of the playa's handbook,

> *...a self-made brother must cook the woman a meal to let her know that he can handle himself in the kitchen just as well if not better than her. It touches their sensitive side and wins major poonani brownie points.*

So, while it is a standard play move, I normally don't pull this one until I know this is someone that I am definitely going to spend time with on a regular basis.

I guess part of me feels that I have known Kimberly for a while; after all, I have seen her every week for four months now. She always seems to handle herself well with the men in the Café. I have seen at least three brothers over the last few months try to make a move, just to be politely rejected. For a while I thought she was married until I heard a conversation between her and Sheila about being single.

I decided on my infamous Lasagna, with salad, wine and cheesecake for dessert. I forgot to ask what she liked as far as deserts, but she said she wasn't picky so I will just take a chance.

Checking the pantry, I see that I have all the fixings for a great dinner. I check my Pandora stations to determine which will be the best for the evening. I don't want anything too upbeat nor too slow, just a mellow groove. I settled on the Robert Glasper station.  An evening with a good dinner and sexy woman would not be complete without good music. I hadn't listened to this station since Michelle accepted the job transfer. The Robert Glasper station was often my go to whenever we had a relaxing evening. While neither one of us was ready for marriage, I thought we had a great relationship and never thought it would end so soon. We dated for two years, but marriage was not in our immediate plans because we both had goals that we wanted to accomplish that a committed relationship would not allow.

We kept things open, freeing each other up to see other people so it wouldn't get too serious. After the first six months, she was the only person that I dated, and I am more than sure I was the only person she dated. Since she moved away, I haven't had the energy to start another relationship.

I decided to cut the night short so that I can get in early in the morning and leave at around 3 p.m. to make sure I have enough time to cook dinner without rushing.

*********************

When I opened my eyes, my first thoughts were Michael and dinner tonight. I won't get a chance to go to the gym, so I want to make sure that I monitor what I eat today, so that I can enjoy my dinner.

Before the lunch crowd began, Sheila came over to me with this smirk on her face.

"Okay, I guess I forgive you," she said teasingly.

"Forgive me for what?" I asked.

"For taking my man, I saw my Tuesday lunch fantasy run out of here behind you yesterday. And I saw you two when you passed the restaurant heading to the parking lot. So, how is he?  Is he nice?  She asked anxiously."

"He appears to be nice. We got off to a shaky start, but I think he is a pretty nice guy," I said with a shy smile.

"So, when are you going out?" she asked giggling with excitement.

"Well, he is cooking dinner for me tonight. Like I said we got off to a shaky start because he misjudged me, so I had to set him straight. Dinner is his way of apologizing."

"That's nice, but what do you mean misjudged you?"  Sheila asked with a confused look on her face.

"He assumed that just because I worked here at Bailey's that I fell into the typical stereotype of uneducated and unexposed. He nearly passed out when I told him where I worked out. "I said in a matter-of-fact tone.

"Oh yeah, the City Athletic Club; I swear I have never seen a more swanky, up tight and stiff gym in all my life. As much as I love to work out, I appreciate my little hole in the wall gym; it is so much less stressful. You don't have to worry about working out and matching. "

We both laughed because she could not have been more right.

The hours seem to go by fast because before I knew it my shift was over, and it was time to go home and beautify. I washed my hair and took a nice hot bubble bath. By six o'clock I was putting the finishing touches on my make up when the phone rang.

"Hello," I could not help but smile as I heard his soft voice on the phone.

"Hello back to you, how are you this evening," he said teasingly. "I am just making sure that you are on your way and are okay with the directions,"

"On my way for what?"

The phone was quiet as though he had stopped breathing. "On your way to dinner...the dinner that I have cooked for you," he said with slight irritation.

"Oh, was that tonight? Michael, I really didn't take you serious, did you really think that I was coming to *your* house for dinner?"

Another pause and complete silence.

"Yes, I did, we confirmed everything yesterday. I don't make appointments that I don't keep Kim," I could hear the aggravation, so I decided to keep the joke short.

"Well then get off the phone so that I can come on over. I have been waiting all day for this dinner, so it had better be good...Ha! Ha!"

I heard a small sigh as he realized I was just kidding.

"You know I should hang up on you, I can't believe I fell for that," he said with relief. "I know that no woman in her right mind could resist having a home cooked meal with a brother as fine as me...so don't be late."

He hung up before I could comment on that remark, so I decided to respond to that when I saw him in person.

The commute was a breeze; I made it there in less than 20 minutes which put me at Michael's 10 minutes early.

"Hello smart ass," Was how I greeted him when he opened the door. "I am glad you think you are fine, but understand it is a matter of opinion."

I waited for a response but instead he grabbed around the waist, planted a quick and tender kiss on my lips and said in the most romantic tone I have ever heard, "I am so glad that you made it over, I hope this will be the first of many dinners we have together."

I thought I would melt. Feeling really silly by my greeting, I just smiled and said, "Thank you for having me over and I do think you are fine. Don't kiss me like that again or else we won't make it to dinner."

Laughing he pulled me in and pushed me against the door as he closed it. Pressing his body against mine, we kissed passionately for a good ten seconds. Realizing where this was going, I pushed him away.

"Okay, you called my bluff, can we eat now?" I said totally exasperated.

"Are you sure you don't want to live up to your threat?" Michael said with a deep sensual tone. "Between your perfume and this dress outlining your beautiful body, I don't know that I have the appetite to eat."

Starting to feel a little awkward at the situation I was finding myself in I nudged Michael a little harder.

"Okay, see this is why I didn't want to come to your home," I said with a little caution and shame, "I didn't want you to think…"

"No, stop!" He interrupted me, feeling my apprehension. "I'm sorry, I have been attracted to you since the first day I saw you in the Café. I had put any possibilities of having a relationship with you far out of my mind. That's why I was stunned when you spoke to me yesterday," he paused in embarrassment.

"I was looking out my window as you drove up and I watched you as you got out of your car and walk into the building. I just got beside myself seeing you actually in front of my door. I promise to behave myself from this moment forward," he said as he placed his hands over his heart.

"The table is set if you're ready to eat," he said as he stepped aside to allow me to walk ahead of him.

"Yes, I am," I said as I began to relax, "can I use your restroom to freshen up?"

When I came out of the restroom Michael had dimmed the lights and lit candles. His condo was small but eloquently decorated, it had a real masculine feel. The décor was brown and black with a hint of tan. There were a couple of nice African paintings and masks on the walls. He had a couple of really nice vases, which I complimented him on.

"These are really beautiful and vases, they have a really distinct design," I said.

"Oh, thank you. I was up one night listening to late night radio; the DJ was interviewing the designer, Lydell Martin. He gave out is website and I went out to take a look and really liked what I saw. The plate on my bookcase is my favorite. It is called *What Stress?*"

He really seemed excited about his art, and he had a great book collection. I complimented him on his selections.

The table was set with a three-tier candle in the center. I had not noticed the aroma when I first entered the condominium, but everything smelled wonderful. We began with a Caesar salad with nice vinaigrette dressing. Michael then served Lasagna and garlic rolls, which was particularly good.

Over dinner we talked about our families. As it turns out we are both from the same area. Michael was the last graduating class from his high school before it was turned into a middle school. I teased him because when he was graduating, I was just entering high school, which was an archrival to his. We taunted each other for a minute and then moved on.

Michael attended Tulane University and received his bachelor's in accounting. I attended Roosevelt University and received my bachelor's in marketing. We shared our memories growing up and talked about the hot spots we went to as kids.

Michael excused himself from the table and came back with cheesecake for dessert. I thought I would pass out, because cheesecake is my favorite and I have been denying myself the pleasure to maintain my weight. He had a bowl of cherries and strawberries to use as toppings.

"I wasn't sure if you liked toppings or which ones you liked, so I got both," he said with a smile.

I guess he could see the excitement in my eyes. I let out a schoolgirl squeal and shouted "Strawberries!  I love cheesecake! How did you know?"

With a proud grin Michael replied, "Intuition."

After devouring two pieces of cheesecake (I am going to have to add another 30 minutes to my gym time tomorrow), I insisted on helping Michael in the kitchen. This gave us more time to talk about our families and get to know each other more.

"Hey," Michael said excitedly, "Five Men on a Stool plays on Wednesday nights at Acoustic Jazz, would you like to go?"

"Yes!"  I replied sharing his excitement, "I saw them a couple of weeks ago. What time does the show start?"

"They have probably finished the first set, but if we leave now we can catch the next two."

With that, we grabbed our things and headed out the door. We made it just before the band came back out to start their second set.

Five men on a Stool is a five-piece band with a jazz violinist Ken Ford. Impressive does not even describe just how good these guys are. Michael and I really enjoyed ourselves. We danced, laughed, and really had a great time. At 1:00 a.m. Michael announced that he had an early meeting and needed to get home. I was a little disappointed because I was not ready for the night to end.

We drove back to his condo so that I could get my car. I thanked him for a wonderful evening to which he replied. "No need to thank me, this is the first of many I hope."

He was a man of his word. Friday night, we went to see Denzel Washington's latest movie, *Flight*. Shaurice and I were supposed to see Tyler Perry's new play that Saturday, but she graciously backed out so that I could invite Michael. Taking a break on Sunday, I didn't see Michael again until Tuesday at the Café. Tuesday morning when I awoke, I had butterflies in my stomach. I couldn't wait until the lunch crowd came in so I could see him. We had only spoken on the phone since Saturday night, so I was a little nervous to see him again. Just like clockwork, at 1:30 p.m. the door entrance bell rang and when I looked up, in walked Michael with a smile on his face and a book in his hands.

Cynthia offered to let me serve him, but I declined. I would have plenty of opportunities to serve this man, in many ways, so there was no need to do it now. However, I did go over and speak to him. We shared a knowing smile with each other.

"I've missed you these last two days," Michael said with a flirtatious grin. "I brought you this," Michael handed me J. California Cooper's newest book, *Wild Stars Seeking Midnight Suns*.

I smiled with excitement, "Thank you, I can get started on it tonight!"

"Oh no you won't!" Michael said authoritatively. "I haven't seen you in two days so I thought we could go to dinner tonight."

"That would be great, where do you want to go?" I asked excitedly.

"Why don't we go to C'est Bon? Is eight o'clock too late for you?"

"No," I said thinking about all that I had to do this evening, "eight o'clock will work fine."

"Okay, I will come and pick you up. What time do you have to come in tomorrow?"

"I am off tomorrow. I am switching off days this week with Cynthia, she has a couple of meetings concerning her bakery," I responded questionably, not knowing where he was going with his question.

"I have to go to Los Angeles on business Thursday morning, so I wanted to spend as much time with you as I could because I won't get a chance to see you until I get back next Wednesday. So, I figured we could hang out a little late tonight and maybe have breakfast in the morning," he said leaving a pause for my response.

"So, should I pack a bag?" I asked seductively.

"You can pack one or I can, it doesn't matter to me," Michael replied with a smile to let me know that we were on the same page.

"C'est Bon is closer to my place, so you pack a bag," I said.

"That works for me; I will see you at eight," he replied.

As much as I hated to end this conversation, I had to get back to work; a few customers were looking a little irritated.

"I will call you when I get off," I said as I walked away.

Michael arrived at my house on time with a cute little overnight bag in tow. He was wearing a pair of white linen pants and an apricot-colored linen shirt, opened just low enough to see the start of the hair on his chest. The man was looking fine!

He was wearing one of my favorite colognes, Sauvage. The combination of outfit and cologne was intoxicating and a wonderful aphrodisiac.

We greeted each other with a hug and a soft kiss.

"Let's go ahead and put your bag in the guest room," I said to test out his response.

"Okay…that's fine," Michael said hesitantly as if he had missed something.

We began walking down the hall to the master bedroom.

"I don't know if I will be able to stay anyway because I might have to leave out tomorrow afternoon instead of Thursday morning. He said to challenge my bluff.

"What!" I turned around with a disappointed look on my face.

"Gotcha!" Michael began to laugh, "You have gotten me twice already. It is my turn to play one back on you. Now where are we putting my bags?"

Realizing that fair is fair, I responded with a punch to his arm, "We will be putting it in my bedroom, thank you very much," I said with a smile.

Grabbing his arm in pain, Michael responded, "Oow that hurt! You have an awesome punch; I think you put a frog in my arm!"

"I'm sorry I can be heavy handed at times. You are a big boy you'll be okay," was my motherly response to his outburst.

Michael stood at the end of my bed and checked out my collection of movies in the entertainment center. "WOW! Do you still have a DVD player?" he said and burst out laughing. He immediately stopped when he saw my expression as I folded my arms to my chest.

"So, you do a lot of television watching in bed?" He said quickly to shift the tension that was mounting.

"Yes I still have a DVD player; all of my favorite movies on DVDs, I like the nostalgia of it. And no, I don't watch a lot in bed, it's an option…mind your business!" I replied as I put his bag in my walk-in closet, "I have some movies in here and some in the den."

"I see you have *Deliver Us from Eva*. I haven't seen this in years! I am a big Gabrielle Union fan; she played the role of Eva well."

"I agree, LL Cool J's performance wasn't half bad either," I said with a smile.

"Don't tell me you are a LL Cool J fan?" Michael said in disgust.

"Admirer is a better word," I said as I walked up to him, "The way he sculptured his body is much to be admired. Look at LL in *Deep Blue Sea* versus LL in *Deliver Us From Eva*. Much to be admired, don't you think?"

"Yeah, I guess steroids can make a difference," he said in disgust.

Punching him in the arm again I said, "Take that back! You have no proof of that and he said he didn't take any steroids, so I believe him!"

"Ow, okay I *know* you bruised me that time!" Michael yelled in pain.

"I'm sorry, let me rub it. I didn't mean to cause you any pain," I said beginning to worry that he may be getting a little irritated with the punching.

"It would be better if you kissed it and made it better," he said as he slipped his arms around my waist and pulled me to him.

I began to lift his sleeve so that I could kiss the injury, but he stopped me.

"If you kiss my lips, I can feel it in my arms."

Understanding where he was going with this, I played along and placed a quick peck on his lips.

"There, feel better?" I asked.

"Not really, it was too quick."

I did it again, but this time he pulled me closer; and what was meant to be a peck turned into a long and passionate kiss. I could feel my body relax as he pulled me closer to him. Our tongues danced in each other's mouths as our hands felt the warmth of our bodies.

"Aren't we supposed to be going to dinner, I asked.

"I have lost my appetite, I would rather keep this going," he said as he kissed me again.

As we entered deeper into our kiss, Michael's hands slowly move toward my breast. When he did not sense any resistance, he gently grabbed my left breast and then my right. I let out a sigh of pleasure and then returned the gesture by placing my right hand on his chest and squeezing his right nipple.

He let out a soft moan. I then began kissing his neck as his hands moved from my breast and began lifting my shirt. We separated long enough to pull the shirt over my head. He quickly removed my bra to expose my breast.

I could feel Michael's anticipation rise as he was holding my naked breast. He bent and placed my left nipple in his mouth as he grasped my right breast. He gently pushed my body so that I was lying on the bed. He unzipped my skirt and slid it over my hips. I unbuttoned his shirt to expose an extraordinarily strong and well-chiseled chest covered with a nice layer of hair and a luscious six pack.

"LL is it you?" I said teasingly.

"Hush baby don't talk so much," he jokingly replied to which I willingly obeyed. That song will have a whole new meaning for me from this moment forward.

Once my skirt was off, Michael placed his hands on my ass, pleasantly surprised and pleased that I was wearing a thong. When I began to unbuckle his belt, he jumped up and immediately unfastened his pants and in one movement took off both his pants and underwear to expose his penis standing erect and ready for action.

In response I slipped out of my thong and opened my legs to receive him. He turned and grabbed his bag to get a condom, my vagina gave a quick twinge as I looked at his wonderful ass and well-shaped legs.

As he walked back to the bed, I opened my legs wider to let him know that I was waiting for him.

Looking at the juices flowing from my vagina, Michael threw the condom aside and replied, "Before I get in there, I have got to taste it, it looks so good."

With that he lay on the bed and began to lick my clitoris. As I trembled in pleasure, he placed his finger inside increasing my pleasure, working inside my walls as he sucked and licked my pleasure spot.

Michael exposed his freaky side by placing his pinky in my ass. It had been a while since this had been done and it was not my favorite; my body trembled with surprise and pleasure. Pleased at my response to his exploits, Michael could no longer resist getting inside. He put on the condom and entered me. He filled my walls as I clenched him with each stroke.

********************

Damn! She is beautiful, intelligent and a freak! I could not ask for more. No matter what any man says, we all want a woman with a little freak in her. Each may have different degrees, but they all want it. I can't believe that I am inside of her, and I've tasted her pleasure. It is everything I thought it would be. Her skin is soft and hot. I can feel her vagina muscles tighten as I thrust inside her. Her soft moans of pleasure fall in rhythm with my movements. I can feel her body tremble as she experiences repeated orgasms.

Not able to hold my climax, I intensify my strokes going deeper moving in a steady and determined pace.

As I get closer to my orgasm, I can feel her body tense as she gets closer. Two more movements and she let out a scream of pleasure as I feel her walls throb in orgasmic rhythm. One of the throbs grasps the tip of my penis mid stroke and I thrust inside as I released a wave of pleasure.

*********************

Oh My God! I can't remember my last sexual encounter. How long has it been…a month…two months…four, yes four months. I didn't realize it had been that long. Oh he feels so good inside me.  My clit feels so hot, every time he touches it I feel like I am exploding. It feels like it is as red as the Hot light at Krispy Kreme, every time he touches it, I tremble with pleasure. When I finally reach my orgasm, I scream with pleasure and delight. I keep working, muscles because I realize he is not there yet. A few moments later his body trembled, and he let out a deep groan and grunt of pleasure.

As our bodies relax, the reality of what just happened began to sink in. Michael planted soft kisses on my neck and ears.

"Look," Michael said softly, "I know that this is a little early, we are just getting to know each other and it may sound a little corny, but I just want you to know that I am hoping and praying that today is the beginning of a long relationship between us."

Feeling as though he was saying this out an attempt not to make me feel cheap, I smiled politely and returned the response, "I feel the same."

I was not going to take myself on any guilt trip. I wanted and needed this sex and that is it. I have been through enough short-term relationships to not have any expectations. Wherever we go from here it will be left up to fate.

"So, should we order in?" I asked to change the pace of the conversation.

"We can if you're hungry, personally what I want to eat is right here," Michael began the dissension to start round two of what turned out to be a night of continuous lovemaking.

The sound of pots and clamoring startled me as I awoke thinking that someone was breaking into my home. I immediately jumped up trying to think of an escape route when I noticed our clothes lying on the floor.

As I increased my focus around the room memories of last night brought a pleasant smile to my face. I went to the restroom and was embarrassed by the image that I saw in the mirror. My hair was a mess, another reflection of last night's passion. I combed my hair, washed my face, brushed my teeth and slipped on my Victoria Secret satin robe.

Michael didn't hear me walk into the kitchen; he was too busy trying to find everything. He looked so cute. As he bent over to look in the cabinet under the sink, I slipped behind him.

"Can I help you find something?"

He stood and turned looking so handsome. He had on a white tank shirt and fleece pajama pants. He smiled and gave me a quick kiss on the lips.

"Good morning beautiful. I had hoped to have breakfast ready before you woke up. Where do you keep your omelet pan?"

"Did you say an Omelet pan? I didn't know that there was such a thing. I just make my omelets in a regular pan," I said with a smile.

"Okay, I feel you. I can use a regular pan, but you know us Chefs try to use the correct utensils when we create our masterpieces."

"Whatever just cook the omelet already. You starved me last night, I haven't eaten since twelve o'clock yesterday," I said, knowing the response that I would get.

"I don't know about you, but eating *food* was the last thing on my mind last night," he said as he started to come toward me.

"Oh no, don't even think about it. I am hungry and need food before anything else this morning." I said as I threw my hand up to block him.

Michael laughed as he cracked the eggs for the omelets in the mixing bowl.

"Okay, take out the pan and let's do this together."

After breakfast Michael and I took a shower and lounged around the house. We ordered Chinese for dinner and watched *Deliver Us from Evil* and a couple of other movies.

"So...is it okay if I stay tonight too...I hope I haven't worn out my welcome?" Michael asked.

"Yes, you must stay, there is no way I want you to leave after that great night we had. I am really enjoying your company."

Appearing pleased at my comment, Michael placed my face in his hands and looked into my eyes.

"You know I am at the age now where I don't have time for games anymore. I am ready to settle down and enjoy life with one person. I don't know if that person is you, but I like the way I feel around you. I like your energy, not to mention a couple of other things," he said with a mischievous smile.

"Hey, this is the time of year that I go to my time share; would you like to go with me when I return from my trip?" he said, shifting the conversation.

Surprised and flattered I responded hesitantly. "Well, I would love to go, but don't you think we are moving kind of fast?"

"No, I don't. I just told you; I am at the age that it doesn't take me long to figure out what I want. I don't want to rush you so take a few days to think about it. I will need to know by this weekend so that I can reserve the dates. I usually go for a four-day weekend; leaving on Thursday and returning Monday morning; I will have to keep it as just a weekend trip this time though. Do you think you can get away?"

"I am pretty sure I can work it out, but I will let you know in a couple of days," I said as I placed a kiss on his neck and moved up to his lips.

"It will be six days before I see you again," I began, "so I think I need to make sure that you don't forget about me," I said as I moved my kisses down his body to his slowly rising erection.

His moans of pleasure let me know that I was going to stay on his mind for a while, which is just the way I liked it.

Another night of love-filled passion caused us to oversleep, causing Michael to almost miss his flight and me to be late for work.

He called as soon as his flight landed and two or three times a day every day while he was gone.

Saturday, I told Michael that I had decided to go with him to Myrtle Beach. He told me he was very happy that I had decided to go. He made reservations for the weekend following his return from Los Angeles.

The week went by fast. I had no idea what to pack, so I kept it light. I packed a few sundresses, shorts, three bathing suits and a couple of workout outfits. We flew up to Myrtle Beach the Thursday night after he returned home.

The timeshare was beautiful. It had a very cozy feel to it and had a similar design of his apartment.

We went to dinner at a seafood restaurant where I ate Oysters for the first time. I have always been a little leery because they look so slimy, but they were quite tasty.

After dinner we walked along the beach and enjoyed the skyline against the ocean. Michael and I talked about our past experiences, those things that we would like to have done better and our accomplishments. We talked about goals for the future. His was simple, work to retirement and travel. I shared with him my idea for a Career Development Center. The center would be a cross functional facility, providing training, conference room rentals, copying service and minicomputer stations for students and small business owners to use. He was excited to hear that I wasn't just going to work at the Café for the rest of my life.

After our walk on the beach, we went back to the condo and did what we had begun to do best. Our lovemaking had intensified since the first night together. We were really in tune with each other and were equal pleasers. We both shared a freaky side that only heightened our sexual pleasure. The Oysters may have played a part, but it was the total atmosphere. We really let go and enjoyed each other's company.

***************

In the morning I was awakened by the sound of the ocean and waves rumbling; Kimberly's hair tickled my nose and heard her soft cute snore. Kimberly rested most of the night on my chest and her leg was draped across mine.

The covers are half on our bodies; I gently push them back to get a full view of her beautiful hips and legs. I smiled remembering the taste and feel of her soft skin last night.

I nudged her softly to get her to roll over on her back. I begin to kiss her breast and run my tongue down her cleavage.

I slowly began to move to what is now our favorite spot on her body because we both get so much pleasure when I am there. She reacted as she began to awake to the feeling of my tongue exploring her body.

She ran her hands through my hair as I traveled her body and offered a muzzled good morning, as though she was ashamed of her morning breath. I came up to her face and began to kiss her to let her know that none of that matters to me. Our tongues explored each other's mouth as we lay in the morning sun.

She opened her legs to receive me, and I willingly entered as we began to feel the pleasure of becoming one. I grind my hips to meet her pelvic thrust. She brings her legs up resting them on my shoulders to allow me to go deeper as the passion burned between us.

The pleasure of the motion caused her to give a deep moan as she pulled my hips in to meet hers. I felt the now familiar squeeze of her muscle around my penis, and I let out moans as the intensity increased.

We slowed down and I asked her, as a change of pace, to lie on her stomach. She gave me a smile as she rolled over. This was her best position; I could tell from her moans from each stroke.

Lying on top of her ass and feeling her grind and meet my thrusts inside, I can't hold it.

"Can I come baby?" I ask.

"Yes, but you got to come like you mean it," she said through moans of pleasure. At that point I go in deeper and feel her body tense as I hit her spot causing climatic pleasure. I keep thrusting inside because I am not there yet. Knowing this she intensified her movements to a fast shake dancer pump as she squeezed those infamous vaginal walls.

As I feel myself reaching my climax, I intensify my moves and she intensifies hers. As I begin to come, I can't help but let out a yell because it is feeling so good.

"Shit! Oh Shit!" I yell.

I can feel it from the tip of my toes to the tip of my penis. As our bodies relax I feel myself drifting off into a relaxing sleep still lying on top of my girl.

*****************

I could feel Michael's body relax as he drifted into a deep sleep still on top of me. I gently pushed him over, allowing him to stretch out on his back. He awakened for a moment and pulled me close to him before he drifted back to sleep. I could really get used to this; I said a silent prayer that this really would be the beginning of forever for us. I dosed off resting on his chest listening to his heartbeat.

An hour later we were awakened by a knock on the door. Michael jumped up and looked at the clock.

"Oh, that should be breakfast. I ordered in just in case we did not get an early start."

"I am so glad you did; I swear I think that you are trying to starve me. Is there something you are trying to say? Do you think I need to lose a little weight?" I said jokingly.

"No baby, you are fine just the way you are," he said as he squeezed my ass.

We had pancakes, sausage, and eggs for breakfast with grapefruit juice. We managed to resist any replays of this morning's love, we dressed and hit the strip for shopping.

I was pleased to see that Michael enjoyed shopping just as much as I did. This is a definite plus. He asked me a million more questions about my idea for the career development center. I was annoyed at first but realized his question re-ignited my energy for really making it happen. I decided that I would start back on the project once we got back.

*********************

Time really passed by fast, before I knew it; it was time to leave Myrtle Beach. Kimberly didn't know it, but she was the only person that I have ever brought here. I had never met anyone that I wanted to share the place with. She was a keeper. We had a good flight back, I hated having to drop her off and rush home; but after checking messages when we landed, I realized that I was going to have to go to work early.

We shared a heated kiss before I ran off to prepare for tomorrow morning. I told her I probably would not see her on Monday but would definitely be in the Café on Tuesday.

*******************

I hated to see Michael leave, but I was getting a little worried that we were too good to be true, so we probably needed a little break. I only hoped that he wasn't having doubts or feeling crowded and the getting in to work early was not an out to get away from me. I have to stop doubting and trust that this is real, I coached myself.

Monday was a quiet day and somewhat of a drag because I didn't hear from Michael at all. He called Monday night apologizing but explaining that he was in meetings all day and had to go to a dinner meeting. I was a little skeptical but tried not to show it. When you have dated and seen the games, it is hard to believe in the sincerity that Michael was showing. Something deep inside made me think that he was sincere.

Tuesday came and I was excited to see Michael, even if just for a few moments. I wanted to share some latest ideas with him about the career development center.

One thirty came and Michael was not there. I began to get a little worried but figured that he was caught up at work. When three o'clock came and Michael still had not come or called, I began to get a little disappointed and the sister girl began to come out.

"Well, I guess he has gotten what he wanted. I am not even going to trip because I have been down this road before, at least this time I got a trip with great sex!"

Just as I was thinking this, I heard the bell ring and when I looked up there was Michael coming through the door with a dozen yellow roses and a smile that could light up the sky.

I couldn't help but return the smile. I greeted him at the door with a kiss.

"I miss you!" I whispered.

"I'm sorry, I had to go by the bank this afternoon to pick up this," He handed me an envelope.

"They were really backed up so it took much longer than it should have,"

"What is this?" I asked confused.

As I opened the envelope, I could not believe my eyes. It was a check for $50,000.

"Michael, what is this for?" I asked, not understanding.

"It is $50,000 to match the $50,000 you have saved. I would like to become business partners with you. I don't know how you will be in my life; I just know I want you there. This way I can lock myself in. Will you accept me as your business partner?"

Not knowing what to say, I just stood there looking at him in amazement.

"Are you sure you want to do this?" I asked.

"Yes, I don't have any business ideas of my own and don't see any in the near future. Who knows, maybe I will be able to retire early once your business kicks off,"

"Yes, Michael I would love it if you became my business partner. Let's go back to my place and work out a few details," I said putting my hand around his waist and squeezing.

"Okay, but we may have to keep our relationship on a business level. I don't know how it would work out if we stay sexually involved," Michael said.

"I politely placed my tongue in his ear and said think about that one on the way to my house,"

***One year later…***

"I would like to thank everyone for coming to our one-year celebration of the opening of the Community Career Development Center. This was a dream of mine that could not have been achieved if it were not for the love and support of my man and business partner Michael Lattimore. Michael, would you come and say something please?"

"Good evening, everyone and thanks again for coming. You know, if you had told me a year ago that I would have such a lovely lady *and* business partner in my life, I would not have believed you. If you had told me that I would have made half a million dollars in a years' time I would not have believed that. But it is all true and we are standing here today as a testament to that," Michael said as he smiled at Kimberly.

"This has been a great year for my baby and I, and I thank you all for that. I look forward to continuing business with you all; but the one thing that I most look forward to is spending the rest of my life with Kimberly Stewart," he says as he pulls the two-carat pear shaped diamond from his jacket pocket then bends on one knee.

"Kimberly, will you become my wife in addition to my lover and business partner?" With tears flowing down her face Kimberly manages a scream of "Yes!" The crowd roars with laughter, tears, and applause.

*The End and Beginning of Forever!*

# *Exploration*

The Amtrak train pulls into the Atlanta Peachtree station at 6:09 p.m. from Savannah. Samantha glides up the escalator looking for her man. David appears at the top of the escalator looking handsome as ever with a dozen roses in hand and tickets to the Color Purple playing at the Fox; both of which he places in her hands and gives her a passionate embrace.

Samantha is surprised by the tickets and gives David a long enthusiastic kiss. David responds by pulling Samantha closer and gives her a full but appreciative hug, the adoration of being together. David is pleased he could surprise her. They get into his E550 Cabriolet and head South on Peachtree Street to the Fox where there are quite cafés near the theater.

"You've gotten a new car," Samantha says as she admires the profile of her man. "I love the color; blue has always been your favorite."

"Thank you! I can't believe you remembered that" David responded with a smile.

"We may not talk often…but I remember a lot about you. You always leave a lasting impression,"

"Well thank you again, I plan on making many more that will last tonight," David responded as he lifted her left hand and kissed it leaving a little moisture behind.

Samantha

Samantha felt a surge through her body and came very close to telling him to forget the play and to go straight to the hotel, but she reminded herself that they had all night to do what they did best; she was hungry and wanted to see *The Color Purple*.

They arrived at the café, two doors down from the Fox. As they relax at their table in the corner of the café, David leans forward and lifts Samantha's hands and begins to gently massage them.

"I really enjoy our quarterly meetings," David begins. "You don't know what a lift from the day-to-day they are. I would love it if I could see you more than three times a year,"

"That would be nice, Samantha responds but you and I have agreed that this works best…no commitment…no ties…just good loving every now and then. I want to keep it right where we are."

"Yes ma'am, thank you for the reminder, but because I have missed you so much this time please believe I am going to get just a little bit more this trip, I am going to wear that ass out…"

"Don't make promises you can't keep and don't get me too worked up or these tickets will go to waste!" Samantha replied.

To seal the agreement, David leans forward and kisses Samantha deeply. They both agree that it is time to go or the tickets would definitely go to waste.

The first half of the show was amazing. Fantasia was a great Celie. Samantha and David held hands and kissed affectionately throughout the performance. A couple of people cleared their throats during a couple of their public displays of affection, but it didn't bother them because they were focused on the events after the play.

During intermission Samantha and David stole away to a bathroom in an area of the Fox that was under renovation, so no one was around. David's company was redesigning the area, so he knew the crew was gone and we wouldn't get caught.

David pulls Samantha close as he drops to his knees and sucks and licks her clitoris through her thong. Samantha lifts her skirt slightly above her hips as David licks with methodic, slow, and deliberate speed savoring every moment.

Samantha pulls the back of his neck and head in deeper as David gyrates his tongue around her love. While David is rotating his tongue, he also rubs his lips up and down on her vaginal lips making Samantha moan with pleasure.

Samantha feels she is near an orgasm and stops David by pulling him up to kiss her. David obliges as they kiss on the bathroom counter. As David places his body between her legs, Samantha pulls his erect penis out and inserts it into her waiting vagina. The heat, the sweat, and the lust of fucking just a floor away from the show is intoxicating.

David pulls Samantha's leg over his left shoulder as he drives deep with long thrusts. Samantha in response leans backward against the mirror and thrusts her hips up to meet his deep penetration. They kiss as the moans grow and the pace quickens. David grabs Samantha's left leg and holds it with his right arm. While David is driving inside her, he raises her leg up to his lips and sucks the inner side. At this point, the sweat is rolling down their bodies.

David peels off his crew neck shirt and tee shirt as Samantha reaches out to squeeze one peck as she orgasms on his member. David, showing great staying power, moves with slow grinding thrust as he feels Samantha's love squeeze and massage him as wave after wave of mini orgasms overtake her body. David moves with patience enjoying the look of pleasure and completeness on Samantha's face.

Samantha looks through passion filled eyes as she realizes that her man has not been satisfied yet. Samantha pushes David back slightly as she turns around and arches her back showing David that beautiful high sable ass. Samantha can see and feel her man enter her while looking into the mirror. David moans with immense pleasure as he enters her as she leans over the sink. Samantha's muscles grind and pull at his penis as David moves with great intensity feeling her pleasure.

Knowing that intermission was ending soon, Samantha arches her back and thrusts to get him deeper inside her to aid his climatic moment. David places his hands on her clitoris to help her get another orgasm. As he continued to move, David wanted to hold off his mounting orgasm but knew that time was running out, so he succumbs and allows the release which felt like an explosion.

Feeling his strong release and the intensity of David's hand on her clitoris makes Samantha come again as well…. Not bad for intermission.

They both clean up and hurry back. They enjoyed the rest of the play while holding each other's hands tightly. To the pleasure of those around them, the public display of affection had stopped but once in the hotel later that evening the passion flowed throughout the night….

As the sun peaks through the window, Cynthia opens her eyes and gently nudges Calvin.

"Calvin…Baby, if we are going to have breakfast before check, out we need to get up,"

"Who is Calvin? My name is David," Calvin says as he places a kiss on Cynthia's lips.

"I know baby, but the Samantha and David scenario is over and now it is back to reality. Ma says she has a dinner date at 8'o clock so we can't miss the train to get back to Savannah.  She was very sweet to keep the kids for the second time this month, so I don't want to mess up a good thing," Cynthia says.

"Alright, alright I'm up," Calvin says agreeably. "So when can I come back to Atlanta to see Samantha again. We are going to have to use her again for another scenario," Calvin says has he places his hands between Cynthia's legs.

"Ooo, I know, David wasn't too bad himself. Where do you think we should go next?" Cynthia asks as she feels herself getting aroused by his touch.

"Well, I don't know about next, but I know where I am going now," Calvin says as he descends down Cynthia's body to her awaiting clitoris,"

Feeling his tongue on her spot Cynthia moans. "Mmm, you go right ahead, we can eat on the train."

As Cynthia is enjoying another round of pleasure, reality taps her on the shoulder.

"Baby, wait!  You have to return the car before we go to the station!" Cynthia says as she pushes him away.

"No, I don't…they have already picked up the car…I arranged for that when I made the reservation." Calvin says as he begins to finish what he started.

"I love the way you always have stuff in order," Samantha says as she lays back for another round.

*****************

"Girl you are glowing!" Monique says as she enters Cynthia's home.

"Maybe me and Anthony should take a trip to Atlanta."

"It wasn't just Atlanta girl; it was the sex in Atlanta!" Cynthia says with a squeal.

"It really amazes me how you and Calvin still run around like high school kids who have just discovered sex. I have yet to understand how you do it," Monique says in amazement as she sees the beaming smile on Cynthia's face.

"It's nothing magical, it's just who we have become. Please believe, the first eight to ten years of our marriage was average. We had to adjust to each other and the kids. We would have the typical marriage maintenance sex. We might do a little something extra on a birthday or anniversary, but that was it." Cynthia says as she remembers the earlier years of her marriage.

"It was about seven years ago, she continued. Calvin and I were up late one night flipping channels and we ran across HBO's *Real Sex*. I can't remember which one it was, you know they have a lot of episodes now, but it was the episode that previewed a lady who owned something like a brothel where men could come and fulfill various fantasies. She had six rooms, each having a scene to fulfill a fantasy; there was a torture room, a room that looked like a doctor's office and things like that."

"Girl no, are there really places like that?" Monique bursts out with laughter.

"Yes! I have since seen other places like it on other *Real Sex* episodes. Anyway, this sparked a conversation between Calvin and me about fantasies that we have and freaky stuff that we had done in previous relationships. I was surprised because we had been with each other a long time and had never really talked about our sexual likes and dislikes. We stayed up most of the night talking about different stuff and decided that we would fulfill one fantasy a month or find something different to do sexually each month. We both got excited and had the most exhilarating sex we had had in years."

"So, you and Calvin are just big freaks," Monique says teasingly.

"Call it what you want girl, I call it enjoying life and my husband, which is what I am supposed to do," Cynthia replies matter-of-factly.

She then stares into space and gets a sad look on her face.

"What's wrong?"  Monique asks.

"You know what they say, give a man an inch and he will take a mile. Just when things are going good with the explorations, Calvin now wants to take it up a notch," Cynthia says in disgust.

Wondering what she could be implying, Monique reaches out and touches Cynthia's shoulder.

"What do you mean take it up a notch?" Monique asked.

Cynthia looks at Monique having shame about what she was getting ready to say.

"You know, every man's fantasy, the ménage a toi," Cynthia says as she drops her head.

"Oh no," Monique says in complete understanding.

"I don't know what it is about men and their need to have sex with two women," Cynthia says in disgust. "I keep telling Calvin that I am fine with just us, but he thinks that this will add a little more flame to our "already hot sex life" as he puts it. He is even willing to give me the experience of two men if I want it. Can you believe that?  I am starting to be afraid that he might be gay. What man is willing to share his wife with another man?"  Cynthia's voice begins to rise.

Sensing her anger, Monique decides to step in and share her experiences to ease her tension a little.

"Wait Cynthia," Monique begins. "I know it is sometimes hard to believe, but there are some men who enjoy seeing their partners get pleasure from another man or woman. The experience can be quite rewarding," Monique says shyly as she sees Cynthia expression change from anger to amazement at what she was hearing.

"And no, it does not mean that the man is gay."

"So," Cynthia smiles, "are you trying to say that you have been with two men? I had no idea that Anthony rolled that way,"

"Well, this happened before Anthony," Monique began.

"I was dating this guy for a few years. I credit him for helping release a lot of my sexual inhibitions. We discussed it several times and talked about it and I wasn't in total agreement, but I was starting to lean in the direction. One day I came home from work and when I opened the door Tony was standing there with my favorite drink in hand. He greeted me with a hot passionate kiss."

Cynthia folded her arms tightly across her chest anxious to hear the story. Monique laughed at her anticipation and continued with the story.

*"I have a surprise for you,"* he said. *"I need you to relax and go with the flow."* I could hear the shower running and he took my hand and led me upstairs to my bedroom. He undressed me and escorted me to the shower, then he said, *"Take your shower and whatever you do, don't come out. I will come in and get you."* Once I was finished with the shower, he came in with one of my chemise that he loved, dried me off and slipped it over my head. "

"That sounds sexy," Cynthia said with excitement.

"Wait girl this is just the beginning," Monique said. "He then pulled out one of my scarves and blindfolded me. At this point I knew what was happening and just took a deep breath. He led me to my bedroom and helped me lie down on my stomach. He then began to rub me down with oil. He was an excellent masseuse, and I was lying there enjoying it as usual. Then I felt another pair of strong hands on my legs as Tony moved to my shoulders. The second hand moved from my legs to my feet and began to massage them. Girl, the next thing I knew I was getting my back and shoulders rubbed and my toes sucked. At this point, I decided that this was not half bad and I might as well enjoy the moment. They rolled me over and started massaging my breasts and legs. The second pair of hands opened my legs and my whole body tensed with anticipation as to what was going to be next. He began to place kisses along my inner thighs, and I began to tremble from the tickling and sensuous sensation. Tony began to kiss my neck and worked his way down to my breast as the second pair of hands spread me open and began to lick my spot. After about the third lick I was climaxing all over the place. We must have gone on for an hour. I didn't know I could have that many orgasms," Monique began to fan herself as she remembered the heated pleasure.

Anyway, I hated to admit it, but that was an impressive and sensual experience, I wouldn't change a thing about it."

"Yeah Monique, at least that was two men, Calvin wants our session to be with another woman. If I do it and enjoy it what will that say about me?" Cynthia asks with fear and protest in her voice.

"It will only say that you know how to please your man," Monique says in reassurance.

"It won't mean that you are a lesbian. It won't be you and the woman by yourself. Look at it the way Tony approached our experience, you are taking pleasure in giving your man pleasure," Monique looks at Cynthia and takes her hand.

"Before you make your decision, I think that you should talk to Calvin about your fears and ask him how he will feel if you enjoy it. Will he think that you are gay?  I think you all should paint different scenarios around the situation and discuss the pros and cons. Who knows, once he really thinks about it, he may change his mind. Whatever you do Cynthia, it will be between you and your man and that is all that matters."

Cynthia hugs Monique. "Thanks Monique, I am glad you shared your experience with me, I think that is the biggest hang up that I have, what other people will think of me. Calvin is my husband. If I had this kind of experience, I couldn't think of anyone that I would rather have it with. We have talked about it and he is very secure and somewhat expects that I will really enjoy it. Not that he thinks I like women, but we have just heard that it is supposed to be a great experience.  I personally don't think that it is any better than what a man can give you if he is willing."

"Now I can agree with that, what a woman can do for me that a well-trained man can't do?" Monique says as she gives Cynthia an agreeable high five.

"Look Cynthia, I have to go, Anthony and the kids will be home shortly, and we are going to see a movie tonight. I love you girl, let me know how things go."

"I love you too Monique, thanks again for sharing," Cynthia says as she walks Monique out the door.

It's been a month since Cynthia and Monique had the conversation about Calvin's request for a ménage a toi. Cynthia has given the idea a lot of thought and even prayed about it. Although she felt a little sacrilegious praying to God about a ménage toi,, Cynthia is reminded of how her mother use to say, *"take everything to God in prayer, he knows what is going on any way so you might as well talk to him about it."* When Calvin brought up the conversation to plan next month's excursion Cynthia just told him to relax because she had something in mind that he might enjoy.

*Exploring in Love...*

# *Invisible Brother*

## *Invisible Brother Defined*

I call myself the "Invisible brother" because I am that rare species that society hears very little about. I'm the brother that holds the 9 to 5 and has kept the same job for the last 16 years since graduating college at the sweet age of 22. I majored in business and landed a job after completing an externship at Lamar Consulting as a Jr. Executive. I have now worked my way up to a Sr. Vice President position. I have never been married, have no babies living or, as my buddy Horace the master gigolo would say, "on a shelf as a specimen,"

I have dated my share of women but none that have motivated me to marriage. I just haven't found the one that I could build a family with, like the one my mother and father did. They were not perfect but we had and still have a family bond that cannot be broken.

Most of the women I have dated fall into one of three groups, which leaves them out of the marriage category for me:

- Completely broke and need a provider.
- Rich and educated but too materialistic.
- Just getting by with no aspiration to do more.

The woman that I will spend the rest of my life with will be strong and independent, yet able to ask for what she needs and support me without feeling as though she is being submissive or losing her identity. She will add to me, not take away. We will share a common interest that will grow and even change, as we grow older together; she will be my friend and confidant.

Now, before you begin to analyze me, and put me in the wrong categories, I am the second of four children raised by both my mother and father. I have one brother and two sisters, which provided an equal balance of men and women in our household. My parents had a wonderful relationship, not without faults, but great in the sense that they worked together as a team and taught us to do the same. Chores were shared equally in our home and as a result, I can out cook any woman when it comes to mac & cheese, collard greens and all meats. Ironing is my specialty, and I can't function in a cluttered home. Let me stop you again, I am not arrogant or selfish, gay, or a downlow brotha. I am who I am, and I thank God for that, which explains why I am invisible; there is nothing scandalous about men like me. As a result, our news and television programs have no interest in us, but rather the ones who are either on drugs or selling them, stealing or raping. I am not in the have-sex-with-you-then-don't-call-back category that some women like or need and I don't have a prison record that another special group of women out there prefer.

The African American bestselling authors aren't interested in me because, to sell their books, they need doggish rough neck brothas like I just described. Add to those characteristics a baby mama whose best friend they are sleeping with and are now baby mama number two. Once again, this is all the evidence that makes me invisible. Don't get me wrong, I don't mind not getting the attention, I just think that it is time for people to hear from us; we do have a voice and lead pretty interesting lives.

Now when I began my story, I told you that I hadn't met anyone that sparked my interest, to the degree of marriage; that is until a month ago when my eyes caught the vision of a milk chocolate beautiful black woman. At first glance, she looked like a younger version of my mother, 5'8", short, cropped hair, well-toned body and a walk of sheer confidence. The one thing I admire about my mom, and what this woman reflects, is that she has always managed to keep a great shape and she has always been confident.

 As a boy I can't tell you how many times I fought with my friends who would be foolish enough to make a stupid comment like, "One day I am going to be your step daddy," or how many men I wanted to jump for gazing at my mother's legs and ass. One day my brother, sisters and I were out shopping with my mom and a man approached her and asked for her number. As soon as I got home, I rushed to my father and shared my anger and frustrations; his reply helped me to put my feelings in their proper place. Being the strong and confident brother that my father is, he simply smiled and told me that the ultimate form of flattery for a man is to catch another man admiring his woman.

"Everything within its limits," he warned, 'but another man's gaze and flirtation with your woman only confirms what you feel inside for her," He trusted my mother, so he never had a need to be overly offended by anyone else's admiration.

The vision of beauty that now captured my attention would definitely be someone that I would constantly catch others admiring.

## *Meeting of the Minds*

The one thing that I used to enjoy after a long work week was picking up a couple of movies from Blockbusters and having a quiet evening at home with some Lemon Pepper wings, fries and Makers Mark. When Blockbusters closed, someone in our neighborhood bought the building and re-opened it as a community DVD and CD movie rental, called Max Rental. When they opened, they reached out to the community asking for CDs and DVDs. The owners paid $1 for DVDs and $1.50 for each CDs. Knowing that with streaming becoming more popular, they knew that most people would either throw away their DVDs and CDs or donate them to Goodwill. They also began taking donations of old DVD and CD players; this allowed them to rent those out as well. It is amazing how vast their library has become. They have a wide selection of classics and some great independent films that have never made it to theatres or television. I have found some great movies that I wouldn't have gotten a chance to see through the streaming channels. They really keep the nostalgia going.

This is where I was that Friday after a hectic week at work, picking out Denzel Washington's movie, *Taking of Pelham 123*. I have seen almost every Denzel movie since his first movie *Carbon Copy*; the ladies love him for his looks-I admired the man for his talent and swagger. I was trying to decide if I wanted to get another movie, when I heard the jingling of keys approaching me. I don't know why the sound stood out, but whatever the reason, I looked over my shoulder and thought I was going to drop to my knees. Approaching me was one of the finest women I have ever seen. She had on a short leather jacket with a black skirt that stopped a few inches above her knees and boots that gave just enough emphasis to voluptuous thighs and legs. With legs like that I could only imagine what the backside was like. I caught myself mid-stare and tried to play it off, but realized it was too late. To correct my stupidity, I quickly made up an excuse to offset my lustful glare.

"Oh, I am sorry to stare; I thought you were an old classmate. How are you this evening?" I asked, keeping my tone casual.

"No problem, fine and yourself?"  She replied as she reached in front of me also choosing the last of the two copies of *Taking of Pelham 123*.

Good she has a warm personality – let me keep the conversation going.

"I am getting the same movie, have you heard good things about it?" I asked.

"Yes, my girls say it is one of Denzel's best and it keeps you on the edge of your seat. I figure it will be a great distraction while I am on the treadmill," She said.

"So, you work out?" I ask as I try to picture her body in a one of those cute fitness outfits.

"Yeah, just trying to keep the body right and fight off the aging process," She said with a half-smile.

"I would say you're winning right now," I complimented while I bit my bottom lip and wondered how her lips would feel against mine and if her body was as warm on the inside between those powerful thighs as her smile is now as she looked at me.

I immediately checked myself and remembered the vow of abstinence that I had just taken at church; I am supposed to be leading a life free of lust and pre-marital sex. Three months in and I was doing well until now - I really need to re-adjust.

"Hey," I paused looking down at the movie in my hand, "I'm checking out the same thing, but I plan on sitting back and relaxing while I watch mine. Would you like to skip the treadmill and watch it together?" I could not believe I just said that! What in the hell was wrong with me? I know she must think I am a total idiot. Damn my stupidity.

To my surprise, she just smiled and said, "Well not tonight but maybe some other time?"

I thought I would shit a brick. "Sure," I said as I immediately began reaching for a business card. "I'm Philip Marshall and you are?"

"My name is Jasmine Cook," she said, smile intact and reaching for a card as well. When she handed me her card I couldn't believe it, she was a project manager at the research agency that's bidding to complete an employee satisfaction survey where I work. They have completed similar projects for other organizations and are in high demand.

"Your company is being considered to manage a project coming up," I said.

"I was just looking at your card and thinking the same thing. I am not on the team that will service the account, but my good friend and co-worker, Horace Walker, will be the lead project manager," she said.

"I know Horace; we hang out at least once or twice a month. I can't believe what a small world this is," I did a double when I realized the implications. Horace was recently married so I knew they weren't currently dating, but needed clarification of anything that could have gone on before his marriage.

"So, how do you know Horace, did you all date? I asked cautiously.

"Horace and I met in college. He was the brother of one of my Sorors, Stephanie, and we hit it off. It was never anything romantic between us, from day one we have always been cool with each other. He is a couple of years older than me and has always looked out for me. As soon as he saw another position open in his department, he referred me, and I got the job. He is like the brother I never had."

"That's cool," I said very relieved. "So now that we know each other you sure you don't want to skip your treadmill date and watch the movie with me?  I gave my winning smile.

Returning the smile, she said. "I don't *know* you, we've been talking for maybe five minutes, that's hardly enough time to say that I know you."

"Well, it's like we know each other," I continued to negotiate. I mean we are both good friends with Horace, so we are half way there. I tell you what...let's get Horace to decide."

Anxiously, I pull out my cell and start to dial. I didn't want to chance letting her leave and never seeing her again.

"I know you aren't calling Horace. What do you think he can say that will change my mind?" She smiles teasingly.

"Hey Horace, this is Phil...you know I can't call it man what's up with you?  Listen, I called because I am standing here trying to convince a beautiful young lady that I just met at Max Rental to watch a movie with me tonight and I thought you could help plead my case because you know her. Its Jasmine man she says you all are co-workers and buddies.
"

I pull the phone away from my ear as he hollers with laughter. "Man you are a trip, Horace says between his laughter. "Put her on the phone,"

"Hey Horace," Jasmine says with a slight irritation in her voice. "I know you are not even going to try to convince me to do this."

"Jazz look," Horace began. "I know nothing I say is going to convince you to do it, so I will just let you know that if you decide to do it, you won't regret it. Phil is a great guy, I feel bad because I never thought to introduce you two, ya'll would be good for each other, you will find that you have a lot in common."

I wish I could have been privy to what Horace was saying to her. I stood there, like a child watching his parent have a phone conversation with his teacher, hoping things would be okay when the call finished. The most I heard was, "mm-hmm uh-huh, okay and whatever."

"Whatever Horace!  Thanks for your input!" Jasmine snapped before handing me the phone and walking off without saying another word to me.

"Oh shit, I think we pissed her off Horace," I said anxiously. "I didn't mean to offend her. Let me hit you back."

I caught up with Jasmine in the line. "Jasmine look, I was just kidding about me coming over tonight and I don't want you to think that I am forcing the issue. I just like your energy and you seem like a good person to talk to and hang out with. I would love to plan a date with you for another night, it doesn't have to be tonight."

She gives me a cutthroat stare; you know the kind that your mother gives you when you have crossed the line. "Okay, this is crazy, but I'm really not feeling the treadmill thing, so I will see you in an hour, here is my address."

I could not believe what I was hearing. She was inviting me over!  She didn't live far from me, which was convenient. I wondered if she shared the same loyalty to the in-store movie rental that I did.

"Great," I said. "I am tired of watching movies alone myself. I was going to get some Lemon Pepper wings and fries; would you like for me to get you something?"

Jasmine smiled. "You know I am starting to be afraid of you, because that is what I was planning on getting, so yes get some for me. I like to drink Grey Goose with my wings; can you bring something to chase it with?

"No problem, consider it done," I say looking at my copy of the movie. Wow, a Grey Goose drinker, I wonder if this is going to be an indication of things to come. I have never been one to spend a lot of money on my alcohol; I always left that to my bourgeois friends. I have always preferred brown liquor, not the cheap kind, but the moderate priced ones like Makers Mark. I will try something new tonight...variety is the spice of life.

"I guess I should put this back, no need in renting my copy now, I will choose another movie, in case we get in the mood for a double feature," I said teasingly.

"Well, I can't promise you that," Jasmine said, with a stern look of *don't push it*. Just then her turn came up to check out. "I will see you in an hour, call me if you have problems with the directions.

### *Is This Right?*

"I don't believe this!" I think as I walk to my car.

I know my mom is somewhere in heaven right now having a fit because I am letting some man that I just met come to my home. I know I should be leery, but it is something about his smile, his voice and the vibe that I get that lets me know it is a safe gesture. The fact that he knows Horace really helps as well. Now I have to rush home shower and get ready. It is a tight squeeze, but I know I can do it. I have to tell Stephanie about this, I know she is going to have a fit. For the last 20 years she has been just like a sister, guiding me through all of my madness. I pushed the speed dial as I backed out of my parking space.

"Hey Steph, what's going on?"

"Nothing girl, you know me I am getting ready to do my typical Friday night date with Lawrence. Tonight, we are going to eat at this new Thai restaurant downtown. He is really looking forward to it but personally, I would be happy staying at home ordering Chinese. So, what's on your agenda...or should I say what movie have you rented tonight?"

"I am watching *Taking of Pelham 123*, but not alone," I say, holding my breath for her response.

"What! "Who are you watching it with and why haven't you told me that you met somebody?" She yelled, ready to ask a million more questions.

"I am telling you now," I say teasingly. "It's the Max Rental guy; we were both renting *Taking of Pelham 123* and this time he spoke to me." I had long before told her about him and had even manipulated my schedule to make sure I was there almost every Friday just to catch a glimpse of him. Prior to today, I had been too intimidated to strike up conversations or even get too close, and I don't think he had ever noticed me. I typically rent romance-comedy themed movies, while he is all action-adventure; the sections on are opposite ends of the store. I don't know what made me do it, but jingling with my keys caught his attention and I am glad.

"Are you out of your mind, have these three months of abstinence made you lose all your sense?  How can you invite someone you just met to your house to watch a movie?"

"Before you get started, hear me out," I say needing her understanding. "First of all, I think there's a reason why I keep seeing the man over and over again, and he is always by himself. After seeing him at Max Rentals the first time, I ran into him at Wholefoods, and I swear I thought I saw him when I was leaving church one Sunday. Second, I already told you the man's fine."

I paused a moment to think about his smile that was so warm it almost made me melt inside.

"Third," I continued, "He's good friends with Horace, and last but not least, I'm tired of sitting at home by myself, and if you tell the truth, you're tired of it for me," I giggled. "There were just too many commonalities to let the opportunity pass."

"Humph," she grunted in response.

"I feel safe," I replied, almost whining.

"Whatever Jazz, I still think you are crazy! I will call you to make sure you're okay. Make sure you let Horace know that this guy is coming over too," I don't believe you! Is he fine at least?"

I closed my eyes to picture him as I gave Stephanie a description. "Girl yes, he is brown skin about 6'4" with nice strong arms and a chest you could easily rest your head on in the middle of the night. He has a nice firm ass so when things get rocky you got something to hold on to."

"Okay, that is fine, but don't forget your vow of abstinence. Remember your re-dedication to God," Stephanie reminded in a motherly tone and hypocritically because she and Lamar didn't even think about taking the vow. They had long accepted their "sin" status in their five-year relationship. Neither Steph nor Lamar felt they were ready for marriage; living together is what worked for them, and I was not the one to judge.

"How long has it been now?" she asked, snapping me back to reality.

"Three months," I said. The vow meant a lot to me, and I didn't want to do anything to keep me from sticking with it. It had been challenging at first, but I thought about sex less and less each day...up until now. I just knew when Reverend Douglass proposed it to the congregation that I would not last more than a month tops, but I have actually made it three so far and it has been great. I have a better appreciation of myself and realize that life and relationships are about much more than sex, not that the last three months had made me an authority on the matter.

As I arrived home and placed the keys in my door, I realized that I really had to put a rush on things, so I ended the conversation with Stephanie.

"Look girl, I'm home and I have to make a mad dash to the shower and get ready. Enjoy your Thai and call me to check in...love you,"

"I love you too," Stephanie said with a hint of discuss in her voice. "Jazz I am not feeling this tonight, but I will affirm that everything will be okay. I am glad you've met someone, and I pray he doesn't turn out to be a jerk like the last three guys you met."

"Thanks for the encouragement," I said sarcastically and hung up the phone. Leave it to Stephanie to remind you of your failures. I'd made some bad calls with a few men, giving up the goods way too early all in the name of false love. I admit that my standards weren't always what they should have been; I was always doing the 'extras' for men who were hardly worthy. Everything from cooking meals every night, to doing laundry, to exploring and expanding boundaries of intimacy that should have been reserved for the man who would give me his last name.

I wasn't denying my mistakes but didn't need Shelia to remind me of them and judge me by them. Things had changed for me. I was going to hold to this vow if it killed me.

## *Confirmation*

I could not get out of Max Rentals fast enough. I had to call Horace and let him know I was going to Jasmine's tonight.

"Horace, can you believe it, Jasmine is letting me come over tonight?"

"What?" Horace said in disbelief. "She must really like you because there is no way I thought she would buy into my sales pitch. Look, my name is riding on this, and I have much respect for her, so if you even try to be a buster about this, I will kick your ass personally."

"Man please!" I said, appalled by his implications. "You know you don't have to worry about me doing anything that will make her uncomfortable or put everything that I have worked for at risk. Besides, you know I have been doing that celibacy thing for a minute now, I look at women differently now," I said as I began to think about Jasmine's smile. "Although I must admit, a brotha is drooling over Jasmine, but I am going to and can keep myself intact. I have no intentions on messing this up...believe me."

"I believe you, but Jazz is pretty fine, so you might have to pull a *Something About Mary* to get through this date," Horace says as he bursts into laughter.

"What is that?" I asked, completely clueless.

"In the movie, *Something About Mary,* Ben Stiller's character has a deep infatuation with Cameron Diaz's character Mary. He is getting ready for a date with her, and his friend suggests that he jacks off before the date so that he won't have to worry about getting horny or pre-mature ejaculation later in the evening. It is a funny movie, you should check that one out on your next Max Rentals visit," he says continuing to laugh.

"Damn Horace that is foul. Why you gon' play me to be that weak? I am pretty sure I can make it without needing to handle myself before the date," I say, beginning to get a little irritated.

"Yeah, you say that now, but I am sure if you think about Jazz and her gorgeous self-long enough and then being alone with her in that cozy pad of hers, you will want to pull out the lotion," Horace barely gets this out as he explodes into laughter again.

Suddenly things aren't too funny as I realize that he has been to Jasmine's house and has a pet name for her, which could imply that there could be more to their relationship.

"How do you know what her house looks like and why is she 'Jazz' all of a sudden?" I ask suspiciously. "Is there something I need to know?"

"Man please, do you think that if I had ever had any of that ass, we would be having this conversation? *Jazz* and I are just friends, she is cool and good people, she's like a little sister; if you get to know her, you will find that everyone abbreviates her name."

The thought of trying to date her never crossed my mind when we first met. She was my sister's best friend, which made her more like a sister to me. I've hung out at her place, and she has hung out at mine…with other people around, so ease up," If you think about it hard enough, I have mentioned her to you on more than one occasion, but your mind was always somewhere else."

"Okay," I said a little embarrassed. "I just wanted to make sure. Well, I am going to bounce so that I can hit the shower and pick up the food...I will talk to you later."

"All right, catch you later, but remember my name is riding on this," Horace says with laughter.

### The Date

I arrived at Jasmine's a little late, not wanting to look like I was too anxious to get there...although I was. Horace was right; from outside, Jasmine had a beautiful home with a perfectly manicured lawn. I could only imagine what the inside looked like. Once I rang the doorbell, Jasmine answered, glancing down at her watch.

"You made it...late...but you made it," she teased. She was wearing a pair of black capris leggings and a blingy tee shirt that read 'fabulous'-and fabulous she was. Her level of comfort really put me at ease. There were no heirs to her, which made her even more attractive.

"I thought I was going to have to watch the movie by myself after all; come on in," she instructed.

"I'm sorry, but you know this is Friday and it seems that everyone wanted wings tonight. I had to elbow my way to the front of the line when I saw how late it was getting."

Jasmine flashed that beautiful smile. "I'm feeling kindhearted tonight, so I will let you slide. Plus, you *do* have lemon pepper wings in your hand."

My eyes did a quick and inconspicuous study of her home's interior. As I entered, the walls in the foyer and up the stairs were painted in a deep shade of wine, with the crown molding done in beige. An array of black and white photos displaying various shots of Paris covered the main wall. To my left was a sunken living room outfitted in shades of camel, sand and wine; a flat screen television hung on the wall above the fireplace, and candles were in every corner, unlit of course. To my right was her formal dining room duplicating the color scheme of the living room.

"This is a really nice home, I love the wine and beige theme," I complimented following her lead down the hall past the staircase.

"Thank you, I am glad you like it," she says with a proud smile on her face. "We are going into the den," she said pointing to a room on the left, "but first let's go into the kitchen and get the food and our drinks together."

I couldn't help but watch the tantalizing sway of her hips as she walked in front of me; I started to get a little warm. Horace's *Something About Mary* comment came rushing back to my mind making me laugh to myself.

"What are you laughing about," she asked, glancing over her shoulder for a split second.

"Nothing," I smirked.

The color scheme of the kitchen was black and grey. All of the appliances and cabinets were black, and the countertops were done in black and gray marble. There was an island in the center with hanging pots above it.

"You can sit the bags right there," Jasmine pointed to the island as she walked to a cabinet and pulled out a couple of glasses.

"Wow, nice kitchen. Do you do a lot of cooking?" I asked, picturing me cooking her breakfast.

"Not really a *lot* of cooking, but I like to have about two social parties a year. I invite my friends over to eat, hang out and play Taboo and Spades. I am also in a book club, so I host a meeting once or twice a year and we love to eat," she added with a little laughter.

"Well, maybe I will get to come to one of the dinners, that is if I can become a friend," I said playfully."

"We will see; it depends on how well these wings and French fries taste and how you act during the movie," Jasmine said with a smirk on her face as her right eyebrow lifted.

I began to get a little nervous because I didn't know if the *behave* was directed to anything sexual. What did she mean by how I acted? Was I supposed to behave like a perfect gentleman or was she expecting me to test the waters. To be honest, I didn't really know what her boundaries were. Suppose she didn't have any? What would be too little; what would be too much? Was she going to call me slow if I didn't try to take it to the next level, or would she be offended if my hands dropped just an inch or two below her waistline?

I cleared my throat then swallowed. "What do you mean by that?" I needed clarity.

"I mean you aren't one of those that talk through a movie or have a lot of questions, are you?" She asked, as she pulled out a couple of octagon shaped plates that matched the glasses and handed me one.

Relieved that she was not referring to sex I answered her question. "No, I am not, thank you very much. I consider myself a movie connoisseur. I know how to appreciate a good film by watching and not talking," I was relieved that she hadn't been referring to sex.

We leave the kitchen and go into the den. I noticed more artwork of foreign cities that I could not recognize on the walls. We enter the den, which is just as cozy and welcoming as the rest of her house. There were beautiful pieces of African artwork on the walls and various sized straw baskets and a huge leather sectional. There was a sitting area surrounded by a built-in bookshelf, which held her vast collection of books. Another fireplace faced the couch but this one was lit; with a 52" flat screen again, mounted above it. Next to the fireplace was a home bar that housed her collection of wines and alcohol.

We settled ourselves on the sofa; I made sure to leave ample space between us. She grabbed the remote and with a click turned on the flat screen equipped with surround sound...every man's dream. Forget a movie, who was playing tonight? It didn't matter what sport, I just wanted to hear the sound. This makes watching TV at home a dream. I spent too much time in bars or friends' homes watching games, so I have never thought to set things up in my home like this; another 'something new' to add to my list. *I had just met her and am already branching out,* I thought to myself with a smirk.

It wasn't often that I'd see a woman with a set up like this. In fact, I'd never seen it.

"This is really nice, this room really has a man's touch," I hint inquisitively.

"Well, she begins, noticing the hint, "I can assure you this was entirely my doing. I have never had a live-in relationship," I have a few married friends with husbands; hanging out at their homes gave me the idea of creating a room like this for myself,"

"I didn't mean anything buy it," I lied,"

"It's alright; I get that question all the time," she waved a dismissive hand. "Now if you don't mind, I would like to start the movie now," she said teasingly. "I thought you said that you were not a talker during a movie,"

"I did," I responded sternly. "The movie hasn't started yet."

Jasmine put the movie in and dimmed the lights. "Now don't get the wrong idea, but I think it takes a lot away from the movie when there are bright lights."

"I agree and have no problems with you dimming the lights," I said with a mischievous smile.

For the next hour and thirty-five minutes we both were engrossed watching Denzel try and manage the high jacking of the train. We were on the edge of our seats throughout most of the movie. When it ended, we agreed that it was a good action-adventure movie, but it was not better than *Out of Time*, which, we both agreed, was one of his best movies.

It felt good sitting and talking with Jasmine; again, I didn't feel the pretense that I feel when I am getting to know other people. I didn't feel as though I was trying to prove something. As we talked, we discovered that we both attend New Missionary Baptist church, one of the largest churches in the area. She attends the early morning 7:15 service, while I go to the regular 10:30 service. I complimented her on her discipline to get up that early, and she laughed as she thanked me but admitted it was more to avoid the traffic during the regular service.

"So, did you take the abstinence challenge, the re-dedication of our bodies to God that Reverend Douglass gave us three months ago?" she asked.

Wow. I was surprised at her frankness.

"Yes," I say with a smile. "What about you?"

She nodded as she bit into a cold wing, and then sucked the tips of her fingers.

"How are you doing with it?" Hey, she brought it up, so I figured I'd ask what I wanted to know.

"Good," she mumbled. "You?"

"I've kept my commitment, knock on wood," I said, tapping my knuckles on her mahogany coffee table with a smirk.

She giggled.

"I have to admit that it has not been *that* big of a challenge," I continued. "The first month was a little difficult, but after that it has been a breeze. The funny thing is that a couple of the ladies that I hang out with haven't called me once they saw I was committed to the re-dedication of my body to God. I thought that was ironic given that men are the ones that are labeled to be the dominant when it comes to sex."

"Yeah, it may seem a little ironic, but we have become more liberated. We are not ashamed to let you know that we want sex just as much as you all," Jasmine says as she teasingly bites her bottom lip.

I felt a slight twinge from my soldier as I looked once again at those luscious lips. The twinge wakes me up and makes me aware of how close we are now sitting on the sofa. I begin to feel the warmth of the fireplace as I notice the flames reflecting out of Jasmine's eyes. Damn, another twinge…one more and I am going to have to jet because I am not going to make it.

"So," I say to switch the question, what helps you stay focused? "What is your best strategy?"

"The treadmill, I have lost about 10 pounds over the last three months, which is a good thing," Jasmine says in reflection.

"Brothas ain't hearing that abstinence stuff, even the ones attending the church," she continues. "I was hanging out with one of the members; we had been going out for about a year. We were not committed to each other, but we really enjoyed each other's company and all," she said with a smile. "Anyway, when we went out a week after the sermon, he made it clear that he was not about to re-dedicate and that was the end of our association," she said smiling. "It saved me from continuing to waste my time with him. So, after that I have just been in a chill mode for the last three months."

"It has given me a better appreciation for women," I add.

"How so," she asked, drawing her feet up on the couch underneath and tucking them under her butt. I had to turn my head for a few seconds to regroup my thoughts. Damn she was sexy!

"I've never been one to dog women, but I've had my share of friends with benefits." A short pause allowed me to gather then communicate more of my thoughts. "Now I look at women differently. I make myself focus more on their personality and mind, getting to know what really drives them. It has really been a rewarding experience."

There was a moment of silence as we looked into each other's eyes. Jaheem's *I'm Ready* from his first CD was playing in the background. I didn't mean to, but I licked my lips. Damn, another twinge, I needed to get out of there or else my three months will end tonight, and I will have to rededicate myself first thing tomorrow morning.

Jasmine must have felt something because she jumped up and began to pick up the remnants from our dining. I immediately jumped up to help and followed her to the kitchen. My legs were a little tight from sitting and the third leg was a little tight from lusting. Thank God she was in front of me. With the jogging pants I had on, she would definitely notice the bulge in my pants. Once in the kitchen I positioned myself behind the counter as I waited for my friend to relax.

Jasmine changed the conversation, asking me about work. I stuttered my responses trying to focus but distracted by her body; looking at that ample ass as it merges in with the wonderful stallion quality legs. Needless to say, this did nothing for my attempts to relax. As Jasmine left the kitchen, I followed her down the hall back toward the den when I saw my best escape…the bathroom.

"Is it okay if I use your bathroom?" I ask in relief that I have found an escape.

"Yes, it's right here," she said as she pointed to the right."

I quickly turned to keep her from seeing my embarrassing moment. "Damn" I think to myself as I close the door. I guess I given myself too much credit. I did the only thing I could do at this point, dropped my pants, and filled the sink with cold water. I had to sober this soldier up.

*****************

Maybe if I cross my legs, I can stop my girl from twitching. I can't believe that she is throbbing like this. Philip is so fine, I wanted to watch that movie wrapped in his arms so bad! And I am ashamed that I was watching his crotch. I was glad the day that Stephanie and I mastered the skill of crotch watching without a guy knowing. Hopefully, I still had it.

I swear I saw it twitch a couple of times when we were talking about the church challenge. I guess I should be flattered; God knows if he could have seen my private area, he would have seen a whole lot of movement going on. Thank God he kept a safe distance, because one wrong move and the commitment may be over tonight.

I wonder what is taking him so long in the bathroom.

****************

God, this is not working the way that I want. I am going to have to end this evening. He is down for now, but instinct tells me it will not last long. *Come on...free your mind,* I thought to myself. I began thinking of things to distract my lust. What was the score of last night's game? Have you paid all of your bills this month?  When is the due date for your next project?  I tried to think of anything that would keep my mind off of being inside of Jasmine.

"Well Jasmine," I say as I enter the den. "As much as I have enjoyed this evening, I am going to have to leave you, the Grey Goose is starting to kick in and I am getting a little sleepy. I am usually a brown liquor man, so the vodka is jumping on me; but I really enjoyed trying something new.

"Oh, well I am glad you enjoyed it. I am getting a little sleepy myself," she said although she looked disappointed that I was leaving. She stood to walk me to the door.

****************

I am embarrassed because I am so wet; I feel as though I have peed on myself, thank God these pants are black. I am disappointed that he is leaving but relieved and thankful to be free of this temptation. As we approach the door, I pray that he does not try to kiss me, because so help me I just might throw a leg around him and jump him. I should not have had the second drink; that always gets me stirred up. Lord, give me strength please.

****************

As we walked to the door, I wondered if I should try and kiss her good night. I knew that if those lips feel half as good as they look the soldier is going to jump out of my pants. As we stopped at the door, I turned to look at her and before I knew it, I bent over and place my lips on hers. I quickly gave her a soft peck; feeling good about the soldier's reaction to this, I placed my arms around her to give her a departing hug. As she returned the hug, I could feel the warmth of her breath on my neck and the softness of her breast against my chest. And as you would guess, my partner in crime immediately rose to the occasion; embarrassed was not the word to describe how I felt. Feeling my strong erection next to her, I could feel Jasmine's body jump with surprise, but then relax as she pulled her body closer to me. We began to kiss passionately as we both exhaled and moaned, a release from three months of abstinence. I gently turned Jasmine and placed her body against the wall so I could press my body against hers and let her enjoy my hardness. She slowly opened her legs to allow me to get even closer. Through our clothes I could feel the warmth of her vagina and got even more excited with the thought of how hot it must feel inside. Reverting to my high school days, I started to grind her so she could feel my hardness. She began to let out soft whimpers as she returned the grind. After a couple of minutes of this I could feel her body tremble as she let out a gasp. The grinding was working for her. At the tremble of her body, I intensified the grind bringing myself to a surprising climax. Having reached our points of satisfaction, we continued to kiss and hold each other, both too embarrassed to stop and look at each other in the face.

"I guess I should be going now," I said softly, looking into her eyes, wanting her to ask me to stay.

"Yeah, I guess you should while we are still able to say that we have kept our commitment."

Disappointed yet relieved that she did not ask me to stay, I looked deep into her eyes and kissed her again. "I don't want this to be the last time I see you; I will call you when I get home, and we can plan our next outing."

With a smile of relief Jasmine mirrored my gesture and placed a soft kiss on my lips. "That would be nice, I don't want this to be the last time I see you either."

We managed to unlock ourselves from our embrace and I turned and walked out the door. On the way home I said a quick prayer that this would be the beginning of forever for us.

*******************

Watching him walk out that door was the hardest thing I have done in a while. I wanted to call him back and ask him to stay and never leave. I told myself that it was just the heated moment that we just had, but deep in my heart I knew that this was someone I wanted to spend the rest of my life with.

*******************

I called Jasmine as soon as I walked through the door. The conversation was awkward at first but we planned to have brunch after church on Sunday, giving ourselves a day in between to regroup. We promised that we would keep this and future dates in public places that did not afford the opportunity for encounters such as tonight. That plan lasted us for the next 12 months of dating.

## Unbroken Vows

Fifteen months of abstinence and a better appreciation for women made me enjoy the night that I finally gave up the vow of abstinence. Jasmine and I had been dating for one year and had become the best of friends. Our relationship had endured a few trials, but we came out loving each other stronger after each. Although we had shared some heated moments, none had ever reached the point of our first night together.

I had fantasized about our first time together and knew that when the time came, I wanted it to be special and memorable. So on this special night I booked a corner suite at the Four Seasons, nothing but the best for my queen.

Once we entered the room, I watched Jasmine disrobed displaying every inch of what I was about to enjoy. I began to take off my clothes as well. Once fully naked, we stood and embraced, taking in the warmth of each other's bodies. I lifted Jasmine and slowly lay her down on top of the multitude of pillows on the bed. I kissed her lips and neck as I moved down to taste the sweetness of her breast. As I took each nipple in my mouth

Jasmine moaned with ultimate pleasure. I then moved down to her navel and lingered there as I placed my finger inside her vagina to bring her pleasure. I am selfish because I was doing this to ensure that the juices would be plentiful for me to drink. After I am satisfied that there are enough juices there, I moved down to her secret garden, as the song so rightfully named it, and begin to lick around her clit. I feel her body tremble with pleasure, and I am pleased because I know that with each tremble there is more juice to devour. After about the third trembling orgasm, I go down a little further and place my tongue inside her hot throbbing walls. As I enter in and out, her screams let me know that I am pleasing her and she wants more.

When she can no longer take any more, she gently nudged me to come on top of her and as I begin to enter, she stopped and pushed me away.

"No, before you get in, I want to give you as much pleasure as you have given me, lie on your back," She commanded.

Obeying my baby's wishes I laid on my back as she mounted me, kissing my ears and moving down to my neck. As though she was mimicking my every move I felt her tongue on my nipples, which is one of my erogenous zones. I let out a desperate moan. Knowing that she has found a good spot, she lingers there moving between each nipple, as not to give more affection to one than the other.

She then slowly moved down and placed kisses on my stomach. My soldier started to twinge with anticipation as it awaits her mouth; she felt his anticipation.

"Looks like someone can't wait for me to get to him," she said with a coy laugh. Here I am."

She holds my rod and places her mouth on it.

"I let out what sounded like a cry for help as she wrapped those luscious lips around my awaiting erection. I could feel her tongue move as she rode up and down with her mouth, taking him as deep as she could while stroking him in a wonderful rhythm.

Not being able to take this any longer, I gently lifted her from my erection and placed her on her back. I then mounted and entered her. It was just like I have always imagined and what I felt the first night at her house. Her vagina was warm and wet. At each stroke her body trembled releasing more juices until she reached her climax.

Feeling her body tremble once again made me intensify my stroke, which brought me to a climatic thrust making my body shiver with pleasure and contentment.

Our lovemaking intensified as the night progressed, both of us trying to catch up on the past year and three months of abstinence.

Each episode of sex was better as I realized that this night was the first of many to come with my new bride and wife.

If being invisible means that I could have this kind of happiness, I am glad to carry the title.

*---The Beginning of Forever---*

# *REALITY CHECK*

Patricia stands in front of the full-length mirror gazing at her reflection through the haze of steam from the shower and wonders how she let things get this far. There was a time when her image in a mirror brought smiles to her face; but today she could not believe what she was seeing.

Seven years ago, the reflection of her 5'2" well-toned body was a confirmation of the hours spent in the gym. Patricia was always conscious of her weight because of her pear-shaped body frame; small at the top and expanding as you progress to the bottom. She never spent any less than three days a week in the gym, five when her schedule allowed it. Now her reflection displayed someone who did not care…someone who had let go…a symbol of failure and defeat.

The majority of the women in her family were short and extremely overweight; they reminded her of bowling balls. She swore, no matter what it took, she would not join the club. Her mom and sister thought she was over-doing it, but she knew that as she grew older it would only be harder to get the weight off…fight it now, enjoy it later was her mentality.

Fortunately, her mindset was beginning to rub off, her mother had begun to walk the track at the local high school and her sister had joined the gym; she was averaging two days a week, but she had to start somewhere.

The gym was where she met her husband, Mark; they were both heavy hitters in the gym. Mark was more resolute than Patricia; he was in the gym consistently five days a week. He was one of those people who were deeply committed; the only thing that probably kept him from his routine was illness or death. He seemed pretty nice; he always greeted her with a smile and general hello, but he never made real conversation. That didn't bother Patricia because she was there to workout, not to be picked up.

Patricia learned early that the men in the gym really don't take women seriously. On average when a man sees a woman come to the gym, he knows that some type of major event is coming up, it's a new year or summer is on the horizon. Most men think that women typically don't make workouts a part of the everyday routine. For that reason, to avoid stereotypes, Patricia makes sure that her game face is on when she comes in the gym, and she is focused on working out.

Her routine is simple, thirty minutes of cardiovascular followed by a total body weight work out. During her early years in the gym, she had been fortunate to meet guys serious about working out and willing to provide instruction on the proper methods and techniques. She began a workout routine with Walter, who became her personal coach and eventual lover. After three years of an on-again-off-again romance, she walked away from him, totally fit and truly knowledgeable of how to stay that way. So, there was not a need for Patricia to ask anyone how to use any of the equipment, she knew what muscles she needed to work and what was required to get there.

No matter what she did, it never failed that occasionally she would get a Mr. Fitness who would mistake her for one of the seasonal workout princesses and try to flex by sharing their knowledge (which was sometimes very limited) and show her how to use the equipment or offer suggestions on working certain parts of her body. After 10 minutes of allowing them to flex, Patricia would eventually stop them and share her knowledge.

"Today I am on the leg extension and leg curl machines to work my quads and hamstrings. Tomorrow I will be working on my shoulders doing military presses and using the shoulder press machine. I typically do about four sets with 12 reps, each with about 75 pounds of weight. What are you working on today?"

That usually gave them the hint that she knew what she was doing and didn't need any assistance. A couple of times this occurred while she was working out near Mark, she knew that he had overheard the conversation because she heard him laugh to himself as he saw the brother walk away a little embarrassed that they had misjudged her.

*****************

Mark was truly dedicated to keeping his body fit and made the gym a part of his life routine. Being overweight was a constant in his family and he was determined not to be in the numbers. Most of his siblings, three brothers and two sisters, were 5'11" and above, which they got from their mother, 5'10'' and father 6'8," the height alone was a contributor of weight. It didn't help that they always ate good being testors for their mother who was a Chef.

Mark had been burned a couple of times by women coming to the gym during those sporadic times of the year when they had just made their new year's resolution, or the weather was warming up and they were shedding the layers of clothes to expose the fat that had been stored during the winter months. Mark had become tired of the "I'm trying to get fine by summertime!" statements. Anyone that is serious about body maintenance knows that it is a 365 days a year job, it's not seasonal. It never failed, they would come in the gym using the same "could you show me how to do this" and "what should I do to get rid of this" lines. After about two sessions of *free* coaching and small talk to find out that their coach was an eligible bachelor, they began throw hints of dates and dinner. While Mark was flattered, his dedication required someone equally resolute. Mark wanted his mate to be on the same page when it came to health and fitness, which is why after about six months of seeing Patricia in the gym he knew she would be someone to get to know a little better.

It was after one of these episodes that Mark decided to introduce himself and get to know Patricia a little better. Patricia was on the lat machine working her back. She was on the last set when Mark approached her. "You know if you really want to put more emphasis on the lateral muscle, you should incorporate another set of the military press."

The look on Patricia's face almost made him burst out in laughter, but he managed to hold his composure. Patricia, not believing that she had to endure two Mr. Fitness in one day was prepared to tell this one where to go when you she looked up and realize that she had seen him in the gym on more than one occasion and could not understand why he was approaching her with this tired ass comment.

"Thank you, but I know what I am trying to accomplish and how to get there. Thanks anyway," she said with strong irritation in her voice. Sensing her irritation, Mark decided to end his little joke and introduce himself.

"Yeah, I know, I see you in here all the time. I just saw you brush off another helpful brother, so I decided to come mess with you. My name is Mark Yarborough and yours?" Patricia smiles and sighs with relief.

"I don't know if I should tell you my name that was a mean trick. My name is Patricia Armstrong, it's nice to meet you. I have seen you in here as well, which is why I could not understand why you were trying to give me tips suddenly. You have never spoke before."

"I know and I apologize, but you know how the whole gym scene goes. I take my workouts very seriously and have found that you have to come in about the business of working out and be on your way. Anything else just serves as a distraction. Believe me when I say, I have noticed you and have admired how you have the same approach to working out." Smiling cynically, Patricia responds. "Yes, I do and if you haven't noticed, you are taking up workout time now."

Relinquishing her response, Mark smiles flirtatiously. "Okay, I feel you, but I would like to get to know you better, are you free after your workout session to go grab something to eat. I don't know about you, but I am usually starving when I leave here," "That sounds good, but I can't go directly from here because I don't have anything to shower with and change into. If you can give me a couple of hours, I will be glad to meet you somewhere," Patricia said, trying to hold down the excitement she was feeling. "That works for me. Have you ever eaten at Café Sunflower?" Mark asked. "Yes, I have, are you vegetarian?" Patricia asked, treading the response. "No, but I like their food, so I eat there occasionally. Are you vegetarian," Mark asked. "No, but like you, I like their food. Café Sunflower sounds good," Patricia responded.

This turned out to be the first of several dates for Mark and Patricia. They dated for a year before they were engaged and six months later married. The two developed a consistent workout routine and found that they had a lot in common outside of the gym. A year and a half after their wedding, Patricia delivered their first born, Nathaniel, who both Mark and Patricia decide to pen Nathan. Not feeling comfortable with taking Nathan to the nursery in the gym, Mark purchased an in-home gym so that he and Patricia could maintain their work out routines. This worked out fine as Patricia was able to get rid of what little weight she gained during her pregnancy and was quickly back to her pre-pregnancy weight. Nathan was a terrific addition to their lives and completed an already great relationship. After Nathan's first birthday, Mark began to miss getting out of the house to work out and decided to renew his membership at the gym. Patricia decided to continue with the at home plan.

Eighteen months after their first edition to the family, Patricia surprisingly discovered that she was pregnant with their daughter Alexis. Unfortunately, this pregnancy was not as easy as her first with Nathan. Patricia gained fifty pounds with this pregnancy and developed diabetes. For the last month of the pregnancy, she was bed-ridden which contributed to her gaining more weight. She had an indelible craving for almonds throughout the pregnancy that climaxed during the last month. To make matters worse, she had to have a cesarean delivery which made her recovery time longer after the pregnancy and allowed the weight to take up residence even longer on her body.

Initially Mark didn't say anything as he saw the dust accumulating on the home gym, because he understood the trauma that Patricia had endured. Fortunately, the diabetes disappeared after Alexis was born and Patricia healed very well from the cesarean. So, three months after Alexis' arrival Mark started to hint to the need for Patricia to get back into her workout program. Patricia, feeling the pressure of taking care of a 21 month and three-month-old, had not even thought of trying to work out. It was enough just to try to keep up with the kids and the house together.

"How could you even talk about working out!" Patricia asked after the third mention from Mark about working out. "My work out is changing diapers, washing clothes, and running behind a bow-legged one year old who thinks he is five!" I know that I am not the brick house you married, but I am not big as a house either. I am still attractive and have a decent shape!"

Not wanting to offend Mark replied. "Yeah, baby I understand and no you are not big as a house, but you are carrying about twenty five extra pounds and for a woman your height, that really magnifies to a lot of weight."

Now really frustrated, Patricia places one hand on her hip and gazes at Mark with a small level of hatred. "So, is that all this relationship is built on, being fit and fine. I am your WIFE Mark Yarborough. That means that you are supposed to love and appreciate me even if I were not as you would like me to be. Remember the vow you made, for better or worse, through sickness and health? What about that?"

Realizing that he had totally offended her but standing behind his feelings Mark responded. "I remember my vows and I do love you for who you are, but I also know that you are better than what you are presenting at this point. I love you and that will never change, but I want you to look better!"

Not believing what he was saying to her, Patricia eyes welled up. As she turned to walk away, she shot a bird and said, "I personally don't think I look bad and if you do, then fuck you and your work out plan!"

This was a debate that continued for the next year. Thanks to the faithful use of birth control pills, there were no more surprised additions to the family. Patricia attempted to work out a few times but would always get discouraged because she no longer felt that she was doing it for herself but for Mark's approval, which hurt. She could tell a difference in his attitude toward her. The sex life that they once had, four to five times a week, full of passion and lasting for two to three hours at a time, had disintegrated to the once or twice a week maintenance of marriage sex. Patricia had lost interest in buying Victoria Secret lingerie and trying to do anything to entice the relationship; she didn't feel Mark would appreciate it, because she was no longer the sexy size five of when they first met.

Mark had tried on more than one occasion to apologize for the statement he made. He sold his membership to the gym and began to workout at home again, so that they could work out together. Any mention Mark made of working out either in the morning before the kids awoke or at night after they went to bed was met with resistance by Patricia. Mark even hired a maid to come in twice a week to free up time and take the stress off Patricia. He cooked at least twice a week as well. Patricia well received nothing, she always managed to find some kind of excuse as to why she couldn't work out. Even her best friend Amber had told her she was being unnecessarily stubborn about the situation.

"Girl if Stephan was willing to get a maid and cook to free up my time, I would be working out all the time if he wanted me to." Amber had four kids, and while she was a work-at-home mom, she had a hand full. Fitness was the farthest from her or Stephan's minds and it did not affect their sex life or how much he appreciated her.

"Amber, you have gained about 25 pounds yourself over the last five years and Stephan still chases you as though you had lost instead of gained weight." Why does

Mark's love for me have to change over a few pounds?" Patricia said with tears welling in her eyes.

"Patricia you and Mark met in the gym. For the first two years of your marriage, you all worked out faithfully. One of the things that you loved about him was his dedication to fitness remember? You said that with him you knew you would always be fine, even when you were 60 years old. Remember how you fantasized about being in the yearly edition of Essence that highlights the women who do not look their age?   So, working out was a part of who you all are to each other, and Mark wants that back; you should give him what he wants girl he is a good man. You know what they say, if you don't someone else will."

Looking at Amber adamantly, Patricia replies. "Well if it means that much to him and the vows of our marriage mean that little, then he can do what he needs to do," Patricia replies nastily. *Famous last words…*

The first sign of Amber's words of "if you don't, someone else will" appeared while Patricia was removing a loaf of bread from the grocery bag Mark had brought home and came across a torn sheet of paper with a first name only and phone number, *Sabrina 678-555-3824.*

When Patricia confronted Mark about it, his response was that it was someone he met at the grocery store and she must have slipped the number in one of the bags. The next event was a faint streak of lipstick on the chest of one of his white dress shirts that he wears to work. Patricia immediately rushed to the bedroom ready to reenact the scene from Waiting to Exhale, where Angela Basset's character burns all of her husband's clothes, she catches a glimpse of herself in the mirror and immediately begins to cry. She realizes that even if Mark is having an affair, while not right, she has provided him with the ultimate excuse. In her heart she knows that her husband would never cheat on her but knows that he could be tempted. Patricia decides not to question him about the shirt. Instead, she goes to her refrigerator and throws out the two gallons of Turtle Tracks ice cream, caramel syrup, almonds and whip cream, which has become her favorite "escape the drama" snack. She places Mark's shirt in the wash, changes into her workout clothes and goes to the home gym to dust it off. She starts with 30 minutes on the treadmill that Mark bought two months after Alexis was born. Tears roll down her face as she realizes how wonderful and supportive her husband has been.

"How could I not give him what he wants, especially when I know I want it too," Patricia thinks as she breathes heavily on the treadmill. "I can't believe how out of shape I am." After thirty minutes of cardiovascular she completes thirty minutes of abs, biceps, triceps, hamstring and butt exercises on the home gym. Still allowing pride to overtake her, Patricia did not tell Mark that she had begun to work out again, she joined the corporate gym in her office building and dedicated forty-five minutes a day to getting her body in shape. She used the home equipment only when Mark took the kids out to get ice cream, movies or time at the park. Patricia kept this up for about a month before she noticed Mark looking at her while she was dressing for work one morning. He had just come back home to dress for work after dropping the kids at daycare. Patricia had continued to wear the same clothes although her waistline and thighs had slimmed significantly over the last month and her arms were re-gaining their definition. When he noticed that she was watching him watch her, he smiled and said, "Hey, is it me or are you..."

Patricia interrupted him with a kiss. "No, don't say anything. I realized that you deserved to have what you want, and I want it as much as you do. I am so sorry that I have been so stubborn. You are a wonderful man and I love you."

"I love you too baby and I never meant to hurt you, but you know my history with obesity in my family and it is a fear that I have. I may not be able to know what it is that we may die from, but I don't want it to be anything that we can control. I want us to live a long and healthy life together. I was just afraid that you were going to blow up and I would find you dead one day from a heart attack. You are looking good. I do not expect you to look like you did before the kids, but I don't want you going in the direction that you were going."

Looking into his eyes Patricia remembered why she loved him so. She gently pushed him down on the bed and mounted him. It had been a long time since she had done this, longer than she cared to remember. She had not wanted to do it in this position because she did not feel comfortable; it made her focus on her stomach and thighs. But now she mounted the man she loved proudly and kissed him passionately. He unfastened her bra and slipped her panties off. Mark was pleased to have his wife back, not so much in body size but in the enthusiastic way that they made love. He gently pushed her off him so that he could slip out of his gym pants and shirt. His erection stood proud and strong as he anticipated making love to his wife without the tension and anger that had been present over the last year and half. Patricia slid to the top of the bed and spread her legs eagerly awaiting her husband. He, obeying, crawled between her legs to her awaiting clit, which he nibbled and licked bringing her much pleasure.

"I don't know about you, but I am feeling pretty sick today," Mark said in between licks and nibbles.

"Yes, I am feeling pretty sick myself," Patricia said understanding what Mark was saying. They paused long enough to call in sick on their jobs.

"Now where was I?" Mark asked, placing two fingers into Patricia's hot and wet vagina.

"We were right here," Patricia says as she pushes Mark's hands from her vagina and pushes him on his back. She mounted him again, this time taking in his hard and erect cock. She moaned as she realized how much she has missed feeling him deep inside her.

"Damn my pride. I can't believe I let my ego keep me from this. The phone number and the lipstick mark were just the reality checks I needed to realize that I was throwing such a good thing away," she thinks to herself. As she rode Mark, it was not long before each came to a climax. They kissed as their bodies trembled with pleasure. This was the first of several episodes that day and the start of a new beginning.

*Fit for Two*

## *Second Time Around*

I pulled up to the house slowly in my brand-new black Range Rover; the darkness inside of it hid the sadness on my face.

The music of Eric Roberson was pumping from the speakers. Although it was relaxing in the plush leather heated seat, I gripped the steering wheel tight with frustration. I sat there motionless staring at my wife's white Lexus RX 350 blending in with the falling snow. It had snowed close to fifteen inches two weeks before, the grounds still had remnants of snow with more being added. Tonight reminded me of when we first bought this home; our friends thought we were crazy to move in the middle of winter with five inches on snow on the ground; but it did not bother us because we had accomplished something that, at the time, was our dream.

Carletta and I met in college, she was majoring in chemistry, and I was following my lifelong love of writing. The only thing I have ever dreamed of being was an author and screenwriter; I knew that I would one day be the black Steven Spielberg. It was a dream that Carletta supported whole-heartedly while we were in college and the first three years of our marriage until her career began to take off.

As an African American graduating in the top of her class, Carletta had her pick of jobs out of college, which would have placed her in several major cities including our home, Baltimore. Her love for the Baltimore-DC area helped her with her final choice of Bio-Guard International, a local manufacturer of pool chemicals.

She started as a Chemical Technician and after three years was promoted to Chemical Engineer. It was her promotion that helped us, or should I say her, buy this house. I didn't feel bad that it was Carletta's money that got us the house because my contribution was purchasing furniture for the house from my savings; after all, that's what teams do, *work their strongest areas individually and they all add up as a success when they are merged as a team.*

From the start Carletta was the breadwinner of the family, which didn't bother her at first. She always told me that she believed in me and there was no mine or hers; it was always ours.

I landed a job with the Washington Post as an Assistant to a Consumer Investigative Reporter; I researched the topics, gathered information and he gained all of the credit. While it didn't pay much, it kept me doing what I loved while I developed my film career on the side.

Two years into her position as Chemical Engineer, Carletta's patience with my career, or lack thereof, began to wear thin. My parents taught me to manage my money well, so it wasn't like there was a strain on our financial situation, Carletta became frustrated because my title didn't match hers. My position was not as impressive as the group that she now hung around.

I noticed that she tried to avoid introducing me whenever I attended her social functions at work, after a while the event that once included family members became events only for co-workers. She became even more despondent and less interested in my film ventures, again it was as though she had lost the confidence and belief in my dreams.

Her frustration was warranted by the two film projects that flopped and caused a financial loss of about $20,000; none of which was her money but was a signal of failure on my part. While the $20,000 was a significant loss, it was not taken from our household fund; the money lost was mine, thanks to my grandmother's belief in my lifelong dream.

My grandmother Essie was the reason I was good at managing money. Grandma Essie was my father's mother and successfully raised four children while my grandfather worked as a Rail Engineer. My father jokes about Grandma Essie's ability to stretch a dollar a mile; they had all that they needed but their wants was something that was given after many chores and small jobs. My grandfather passed when I was twelve and left her a considerable amount of money that, to this day, neither my father nor any of his siblings knew the amount. Soon after my grandfather's passing, my father moved her into our home, he could not stand the thought of her living on her own.

When I turned twelve, she placed $100 in a checking account for me and as I would do chores for her during the summer. She would pay me, then take me to the bank to deposit the majority of what I earned; she paid me $20 to help with her laundry and complete other chores around the house; and of that $15 money was deposited in the bank. When I asked for a video game or money for the skating rink or movies, she would take me to the bank to make a withdrawal. I had to record my withdrawals and deposits in my check ledger, which she would check periodically. By age 16, I had nearly $2,000 in my checking account, you could not tell me anything, I thought I was the richest 16-year-old on the block.

Grandma Essie passed during my senior year of college. Because I was the oldest and the favorite of her five grandchildren, she had a separate life insurance policy where I was the sole beneficiary, she believed that the $60,000 she left would assist me in achieving my dream. She made me promise on her deathbed that I would only use the money for that. Carletta and I both agreed that we would stick with that commitment, and we did, which was another reason why I made sure that I managed my money well, making sure I always had something to contribute to our home. I never thought the day would come when I would not be allowed in this place that once meant so much to us.

As I waited for Carletta to come out of the house, I noticed an older model 300 ZX parked behind her Lexus. I wondered to whom it belonged, but I knew it was no longer my concern.

I continued looking at the old four-bedroom snow covered Fort Washington, Maryland home, missing it badly. I remembered us getting a kick out of learning when we bought the home that it was built the same year she was born, 1973.

I couldn't help but notice the smoke coming from the fireplace where we shared our love for each other as the logs burned to nothing; where we conceived our daughter Talina who was now six. The lights were off as they used to be during our intimate moments; I could only wonder if the owner of the 300 ZX was experiencing the same pleasures.

I rolled down the window and smelled the smoke from the burning fireplaces in the neighborhood; it was quiet as usual. I rolled the window up and turned off the car to face what I had been dreading since I drove up. Suddenly I grew nervous about knocking on the door of my home as though I had never lived there.

I got out of the Rover, I could hear the slight breeze pick up, but I was warm in my red and black motorcycle jacket. As I headed for the front door, I noticed a man who appeared to be in his late twenties, coming out of the side door, taking the trashcan on wheels to the curb. We exchanged curious looks as we noticed each other, both of us wondering who the other was.

He was a thin, brown skinned guy wearing a wife-beater T-shirt, jeans and sneakers under a fleece housecoat. I remembered buying that very same trashcan he sat on the curb from the dollar store a year and a half ago. Hate started piercing through my heart as I watched this man empty trash from my home. To make things worse, this idiot was looking at me as if I were a stranger visiting *his* home.

I stood there a moment in shock that another man was coming out of my home, when the divorce wasn't even final; life can be a bitch sometimes. As I turned to walk to the door, Carletta strolled out of the house, in her sweats and fluffy slippers. She was carrying a box with the last of my things in it.

Carletta was a cute, chocolate honey that stood about 5'6", with her hair braided down her back. She had that same dry, cold look she always sported when she had nothing to say to me. I could tell right away this was the guy I caught her on the phone with a few months before our separation; they were too comfortable to have been newly dating each other.

Carletta sat the box down on the ground at my feet, carrying it like she wanted me to leave at once. I caught her and dude looking at my Range Rover; I figured they were wondering how I could afford it; I guess she told him of my lack of money. I had not told her that Random House had picked up my novel and I had just signed a three-book deal with a nice advancement. I was no longer carrying the broke writer title she had branded on me of for the last three years; so much for marrying a brother for better or for worse.

I gave Carletta a disappointed glare. I couldn't believe she had a guy in the house already, especially in front of Talina. She told me when she got me thrown out, it was *her* house, but Talina is our daughter. Now that my finances were better, I would be seeking full custody of Talina; we had a better relationship than she and Carletta and I was not going to allow her to bring men around my daughter.

"All the rest of your stuff is in the box," she said in her cold, bland voice.

Carletta rolled her eyes and she and dude strolled back into the house. I stood there a moment, looking at them and the house, trying to control my rage. I picked up the box and put it in the back of the Rover. I got in, started up and drove off; mad as hell, hurt and at a loss for words.

As I drove home a small feeling of joy replaced my feelings of hurt as I thought of my home. The first thing I did with the money from my book advance was buy a home. The slump in the market has made buying prime for those who could afford it and thanks to the book deal, I am one of those people. Now that I have reached a portion of my dream, I can utilize the money Grandma Essie as a source of income along with my book royalties.

While my new home was not as large as the one Carletta and I shared, it was just the right size for Talina, and me with a fireplace just as nice. I may not have someone to curl up with now, but I could still enjoy the comfort in curling up alone. As I walked in the door from the garage, I noticed my bags for the long-awaited winter weekend getaway. I was hoping that I would be able to enjoy myself enough to forget the drama of the divorce and celebrate my book deal. Anything to get me away from the depression I was suffering thinking about my wife.

The next morning, I drove down the snowy Washington/Baltimore Parkway, with a lot on my mind and still feeling depressed from the previous night. I was jamming to the sounds from my Juvenile CD and trying to shift my thoughts to the weekend getaway. I had heard lots of great things about the resort and knew there would be a lot of women on the trip, so I made sure that I dressed to impress. I had on my dark gray Polo ski jacket, a black Polo turtleneck sweater, my Sean John Jeans and my butter Tims; dressing my best always managed to lift my spirits.

I was wondering just how this trip was going to turn out. This was a trip that my best friend Jeff Marks organized every year, so I wouldn't know anyone other than him. He had tried to get Carletta and me to attend for several years but the crowd was not on her level.

People were driving cautiously in the snow, which made traffic a little heavy. As I passed the Anacostia exit, I thought about all the fun I had plan to have on the trip.

As I pulled into the parking lot of Capital Plaza Mall, there was a large crowd of people waiting at the entrance. There were people parking their cars and getting out with bags packed for the weekend. Some were in groups, laughing and talking. Some were standing, freezing from the cold. Everyone was waiting for the buses to arrive so that they could get on to at least keep warm. One of the things I noticed right away was lots of fine women standing around. It sounded like a thousand people were talking although it was only about two hundred people. I was starting to get a little excited and ready to party.

I parked and got out and walked toward the crowd. I spotted Jeff standing and talking to two women who was facing him with their backs to me. As I approached them, the one on his right turned and I caught a glimpse of her profile.

"OH MY GOD," I thought. He was talking to Vicky and Patria. Patria had to be one of the most beautiful women in the WORLD, I would've bet my life on it.

I met Patria at one of Jeff's house parties two years ago. Carletta was doing her anti-social thing she did whenever I was around my friends; she would always find a corner to sit in and read a book or talk on the phone. Determined not to let her steal my moment, I went to play pool, and that is where I met Patria.

The ladies had managed to take over the pool table which left the guys sitting around watching, getting a full view of ass as they leaned over the table. I noticed Patria when "Second Time Around," an old Shalimar song, came on and she jumped up and began singing. It was really funny because she really couldn't sing, but the excitement in her trying was cute. After the song went off I walked over and complimented her on a great performance, she laughed and punched me in the arm because she knew I was being cynical.

"Stop playing, you know I can't sing, but I don't care because that is my jam," she said as she adjusted her skirt.

"I know, but you get an A for effort. You were singing like a professional, you just lacked the sound," I said boldly and laughed.

"It is all relative, there are a lot of performers who really can't sing but it's the emotions that carry them," she retorted.

"You may have a point, but I have never seen anyone have your kind of energy, kind of a looney, cute combination," I said.

"Oh, so I am crazy now? I am Patria, what's your name? At least get to know me before you call me crazy," she said jokingly.

"I am Ahmad Taylor, but my friends call me EJ, I am very pleased to you…crazy and all," I said jokingly.

"Well, I would like to hear you blow a few notes, so I can put you in the crazy club with me," she said.

"Naw, I won't be in the crazy club, but I will spare you, I don't want to get you all warm inside; I have been known to make a woman or two fan from my singing," I said teasingly.

"Oh so you can sing, I guess that is why you are talking about my singing because you can, or think you can," Patria said as she placed her hands on her hips.

"No, you were the one who said you couldn't sing, I just agreed," I said as I bust out laughing."

"Well never mind, it is my turn to play, it was good meeting you, maybe I will hear you sing one day," she said as she turned to the pool table.

"Maybe you will, it was good to meet you too," I said thinking to myself how much I would love to sing to her while we had passionate sex.

That was about two years ago, Jeff didn't mention that she would be here, but I am really glad. I cleared my throat in anticipation of singing a few bars this weekend as I walked up to greet Jeff and the ladies.

"Good morning, you guys ready to take off?" I said as I walked up behind the ladies.

"We are ready if you are! What's up EJ?" Jeff said as he reached between Patria and Vicki to take my hand and pull me to him for a brotherly hug.

"I am ready and thankful too, Vicki said as Jeff and I released each other, "I did not want to ride on that bus will all those people, thank you EJ for driving us up there!"

"I agree EJ," Patria said as she stretched out her hand, "you probably don't remember me, but we met…"

"Yes, I remember you Anita Baker, how could I forget all that energy and beautiful singing," I said with a cynical smile.

"Okay, so you got jokes, I am glad you remember me and the name is Patria, not Anita Baker, smart ass!" Patria said as she threw up her hand and turned her back.

"Oh come on, you know I am just playing with you," I said as I walked around to face her, "I have thought of you often since we met, how could forget someone as nice and fun as you?" I said as I was hoping to win some brownie points.

Folding her arms across her ample chest, Patria looked me up and down with a sassy smile and said, "Keep going, flattery gets you everywhere."

I burst out laughing and said, "Well that is good to know, I will keep that in mind as the weekend progresses."

Sensing our heavy flirtation and obvious attraction for each other, Jeff interrupted and said, "Okay the buses have finished loading, let's hit the road so you two can get a room."

We all laughed and made our way to the truck; this was going to be an interesting ride.

Vicki and Jeff climbed in the back, which left Patria and I in the front. I didn't mind because it would give us a chance to get to know each other better.

"Okay you two we are not in High School anymore so please no heavy kissing and fondling back there, I don't want any reminisces of affection left on my seats," I ordered as I drove off, "Two hours is a long time for two heated individuals to be cooped up in a car."

"Man just drive and keep your eyes on the road, what goes on back hear is between me and my baby," Jeff teased.

"It won't be too much going on because I am getting a nap, we are supposed to go hiking before the Pajama party tonight and I want to be ready and full of energy to do both," Vicky said as she curled up with Jeff, "wake me when we get there."

"I am not going hiking this afternoon," Patria said, "I just want to curl up and watch my Firestick with my Goose before the Pajama party tonight, I will go hiking with the group in the morning."

"Oh, you brought your Firestick, I didn't think to bring mine. What movies are you watching and are you planning on sharing that Goose," I asked.

"I was planning on watching *Ted* and *The Butler*, I heard they are both good; I could use some comedy and good drama right now. The sharing depends on how much money you have. A sista is in the middle of a divorce so money is scarce," Patria said with a dry laugh.

"I have seen *Ted* and it is pretty funny but I haven't seen *The Butler*. If you don't mind me watching them with you, I can pay you for some Goose, I am a Tito's man myself and have a gallon size that I can share. I am in the middle of a divorce as well, so I brought the gallon size intending to do major damage this weekend."

Looking at me as though she thought I was joking, Patria asked, "Are you really going through a divorce?  That is a crazy coincidence. "So, what happened in your marriage, if you don't mind me asking?"

"I don't mind you asking," I said with exhaust, "I think we just outgrew each other, and she got tired of waiting for me to reach my dreams."

"Wow," Patria said, "what dreams were you trying to reach?"

"I am a writer, have been once since I have been able to hold a pencil. I have always dreamed of writing screenplays and novels; it took a while to happen, but I have just signed with Random House."

"Congratulations!  Too bad your wife couldn't hold on until you reached your goals. What is she saying now that you have a deal with Random House?'

"She doesn't know and if she did, I don't think it would matter," I said with disappointment, "Now it's your turn, what happened in your marriage?"

Patria let out a long sigh before she began, "He turned cold and dry. He let his successful career get the best of him and I became second in his life."

"I can relate to that, I don't understand how people become defined by their careers," I said, "It's great to be proud of your success, but to allow it to dominate your thinking and separate you from those who have supported you is sad."

"Yes, it is," Patria agreed and shook her head as she seemed to reflect on her relationship.

"Okay, let's stop right now, I think we both came to forget our troubles so let's put all of this behind us and concentrate on having a great weekend," I said convincingly.

"Agreed, it will be behind us sooner than we think, no worries," Patria confirmed.

For the remainder of the ride, we talked more about our past. She asked me stories about my writing. I had not shared my art with anyone in a long time; talking with her reminded me of the college days when Carletta and I would spend time together and talk about our plans for the future. It felt good to share my thoughts with someone.

The more I talked with Patria the more I liked her, she was a highly intelligent woman with a great personality. She was a CPA for a major law firm and doing very well for herself. It is rare to find a successful black woman without a huge ego…so refreshing.

I followed all three buses down Highway 70 to Morgantown Virginia; during the last hour of the trip Patria dosed off so I was left driving while everyone slept, which was a good thing because it gave time to think and plan for my future. The conversation with Patria gave me hope that I would be able to move past this phase of my life and meet someone that I could share my dreams with and who would support me in my ventures. It would be great if she were the one, but if not her I know there is someone for me. I was feeling good, it had been a while but it's here.

When we arrived at the Lakeview Resort & Spa, it was all that I imagined. The cottages and condos were lined throughout the property in an L-shaped formation, and way up behind them was an array of colors of red, green and yellow flags waving throughout the village.

People were rushing off the buses, waiting for the bus drivers to open the compartment so they could get their luggage out. Everyone was laughing and talking; you could tell from the energy that they couldn't wait to start partying.

Jeff and I dropped Patria and Vicky at their cabin then headed up the hill to ours. The hike was in an hour which gave Jeff time to get to the room and change clothes, while I found something to do.

When we reached our cottage, I got out of the Rover and just stood there a moment looking around at the snowy mountains around me. It all looked like something out of a beautifully shot photo; everything was a glistening and almost blinding white. It was the most beautiful view. The cottage was spaced off from the other few and looked like a modern day log cabin.

When we entered, the cottage interior had a swank design and structure. It smelled as if wood had been burning in the fireplace already; I loved that smell. The fireplace sat in the middle of the room with cream plush sofa and love seat on one side and the dining area on the other. A flat screen TV and Bose sound system was mounted in its grey, black, and brown rock structure. On the floor in front of the fireplace was a traditional brown bear rug; I have always fantasized about making love on one of those. I grinned to myself as I grabbed my bag and went to my room; I couldn't wait to build a fire; this was going to be a great weekend.

I unpacked in no time. I went into the garage to lift the door so I could put my Rover inside, protected from the snow. I found a pre-lit log and wood to light the fireplace. I fixed myself a drink, started the fire and began to watch ESPN until it was time to watch movies with Patria.

The loud knock on the door startled me out of my sleep. I looked around but did not recognize my surroundings, I didn't know if I was dreaming or if this was real. Hearing the knock again brought me back to reality and I realized that I must have dozed off; the clock on the wall confirmed that I had been sleeping for almost an hour.

I jumped up to answer the door. Patria was standing there with her hand on her hip looking a little frustrated.

"Hey, I am so sorry, I began to explain, "I put some wood on the fire, had a couple sips of my drink and that was all she wrote," I laughed nervously.

Patria expression turned to a smile as she pushed past me and entered the cabin.

"Yes, I heard you were up here calling hogs," she laughed, "When Jeff came to get Vicky he said you were up here knocked out!"

"So, you all were down there talking about me?" I asked, feeling more relaxed that she wasn't upset.

"We laughed at you, and I decided to come up here and wake your ass up! You promised me that you were going to share your Titos, and I was not going to let tiredness keep me from it. So, where is it at?" she said as she walked to the kitchen. "We will drink that tonight and the Grey Goose tomorrow," she continued as if she is overseeing everything.

"Well, I am glad you understand, I know it was just a two-hour drive, but I was little drained. I have been running around this week and not getting any rest. It is like my brother says, *If you don't find a nap, the nap will find you.*"

"That is true, Patria said, "Now where is the Titos? Which one of the movies do you want to watch first, *Ted* or *The Butler*?"

"I will let you decide," I said as I walked to her in the kitchen, "You go ahead and put in the movie, and I will fix your drink. Do you need a chaser or just put it on ice?"

"Add pink grapefruit juice please. Do I look like I can drink it just on ice?" she asked.

"You never know, I have learned that you can't let the cuteness fool you, some ladies can really put it down," I said.

"Well, I am not one of them, so come on in here and sit down the movie is starting," she ordered.

"Yes, ma'am, whatever you say," I said as I handed her the drink. I was really feeling like we had a future, if nothing popped off between us, I knew she would always be a friend that I would want to have.

Two hours later we were sitting on the bear rug eating sushi that we had ordered from the restaurant, talking about the highlights of The Butler. Patria loved Oprah's role, especially when she slapped her son. We both agreed that we needed the laughter of *Ted* to lift our spirits. It was sad realizing that our struggle for respect was still prominent.

I kept the fireplace going; that along with the setting sun shining through the picture window behind us really gave the room a cozy feel. Patria and I continued our conversation from our trip up here. Although we promised that we would not think about our failed marriages, we each shared a little more about the good and the bad and our plans for the future. We both agreed that committed relationships were the furthest from our scope right now. We exchanged phone numbers and email addresses and accepted each other as friends on Facebook. Okay, I am locked in now, no way was I letting go of this energy; I truly needed someone that I could hang out with and share my ideas.

Our conversation was suddenly interrupted when Jeff and Vicky burst through the door from their hiking trip. It seemed they worked up some sexual energy during the hike because they ran straight to the bedroom and slammed the door without acknowledging me or Patria. We looked at each other and laughed as I stood up to take our dishes to the kitchen; Patria got up and followed me.

The first loud moan was confirmation of what we both knew was taking place in the bedroom.

"I don't know about you, but I do not want to know them like this," Patria said as she picked up her purse.

"I don't either," I replied, "Do you mind if I grab my clothes for the party tonight and hang out with you until it starts? Your cottage is closer to the event anyway."

"No, I don't mind, there is more than one shower, and we can watch *Ted* until it's time for the party," she replied.

"Okay, let me grab my things." I was glad that she felt comfortable with me, and I was even more pleased that some of the sexual attraction that I had earlier wore off, more of a sign that we were going to be great friends.

*Ted* turned out to be a funny movie, Patria was a little on the fence and could not decide if she really liked it. It was around nine o'clock when the movie ended, so we both went to our respective rooms to dress for the party.

I threw on my pajamas - which was only Sean John sweatpants, T-shirt and slippers, Patria wore a hot pink Victoria Secret sleepwear with the word *Pink* across her butt. She was looking good; I was glad to be in the role of her date for the party. While I am feeling a friendship brewing, I am still a man, so I am not going to completely cancel out being able to tap that ass.

The set up for the party was nice, there was plenty of food, the comedy show was great and there was a DJ and a live Go-Go band Rare Essence. After the comedians did their thing we partied hard and had a wonderful time.

After Essence finished their set, we took the party back to the mine and Jeff's cottage. Patria and I resumed our positions on the sofa in front of the fireplace, while Vicky and Jeff sat on the love seat. We were all exhausted, everyone was sitting motionless, basking in the fun of the first night. Jeff connected his iPhone to the Bose system and had soft music playing, he and Vicky seemed to be warming up for their round two, Jeff was rubbing her feet while she moaned in pleasure.

We were all sipping on glasses of Titos and grapefruit juice. The glow of the fireplace in the dimly lit room was a definite catalyst for a sensual night.

Patria kicked her slippers off, and had her legs and feet stretched out close to the fireplace, getting them warm. The soft sounds of the music and the cracking of the burning wood motivated me to do the same.

"This fireplace feels so good," Patria said, staring into the fire, "I dream of having a house with a fireplace one day."

"Well," I said as I put another log into the fireplace, "You're a very bright young lady. I'm pretty sure you'll get there."

"I hope so," she said in sort of a sad way.

Patria's cell phone started to ring. She pulled it out of her purse and looked at the number on the caller ID with a disgusted look.

"Yeah," she said as her voice raised, "Nothing why?"

Then Patria's face turned to rage. I started to get worried, we were enjoying ourselves and I didn't want anything to interrupt that.

"You know what? I'm getting ready to hang up on you! I told you I was going away this weekend and would handle that when I get back!" She stood and placed her hand on her hip and began pacing, "You don't bother me anymore Sean, so stop trying to intimidate me with your threats of attorneys! I don't want a damn thing from you other than to be completely done with you! Now, DO NOT call me anymore this weekend, I will call YOU when I return! Goodbye!"

It was obvious that Sean was her husband.

Patria turned her cell phone off and slammed it back into her purse. After witnessing that tongue-lashing, I was scared to say anything. Poor Patria. She could not fight the tears. She covered her face with one hand, and they started gushing down her cheeks. Vicky looked over at her with concern.

"Patria, are you okay?" Vicky asked.

"Yeah," said Patria, quickly getting herself together, "I'm all right."

Then she turned to me as she wiped away tears. "Could you take me back to my cottage please?"

I was so disappointed by her request I was ready to cry my damn self. I had Patria in a good and relaxed mood, we had both managed to forget about our problems for the night; now she wanted to leave.

As we headed out the door, I knew I had to think of something fast to keep Patria from leaving. I tried to explain to her that she was being unfair to herself by letting her husband get his wish by ruining her weekend.

We stood by the Rover while she gave that some thought. After twenty minutes in the cold, Patria cooled down and decided to come back into the house for one more drink.

When Patria and I walked back into the house we noticed that Jeff and Vicky had disappeared; we looked at each other and burst out laughing.

"Let me take you back to your cottage, I can only imagine the sounds that are about to come from that room after a night of drinking and dancing," I said.

Patria had a look of disappointment in her eyes when I mentioned leaving, "Yeah, I guess I should go so you can get some sleep, we do have to go hiking in the morning."

"Oh, I forgot about that, it is pretty late," I said hesitantly, "Do you think you will be okay in the cabin by yourself?"

"Well, I am sure I will, but I didn't want to stay by myself; we are in the secluded woods, Jason could be lurking," she said with a laugh.

"I don't know if Jason is lurking, but if you would be more comfortable staying here, you can sleep in my room and I will stay down here, I love sleeping by the fireplace."

"I wouldn't ask you to do that," Patria said as she put her hand around my waist, "I don't mind sharing the bed with you if you don't mind."

I placed my hand around her waist and pulled her close to me, "I don't mind at all," I said as I placed a gentle kiss on her lips.

Patria and I strolled into the bedroom. It was a nice size room. I could tell Patria was impressed by the way she was looking around. It had a queen-size bed with two bedside tables. There was a small gas fireplace. A mounted 32-inch TV, and a small bar, where I had my liquor already set up. My bathroom was off to the side, you could see the Jacuzzi from the door entrance.

"Patria, you're welcome to relax," I told her as I turned on the TV, "I am glad you decided to stay and even gladder you didn't make me sleep on the sofa."

Patria sat on the bed and began taking off her shoes as I turned on the gas fireplace so that the room could begin to warm up a little.

"I am going to get in the Jacuzzi; do you want to get in with me? I could use a little relaxation how about you?" she asked seductively.

"That sounds good, let me get it started," I replied as I went into the bathroom.

There was a Lavender scented candle by the Jacuzzi. I lit it so that the aroma would add to our relaxation.

Patria followed me into the bathroom and grabbed the terrycloth robe from behind the door and went back to continue to undress.

"You don't need that robe, I promise not to jump you," I assured her.

"I am not worried about you jumping me, but I am worried about freezing, it's still cold in here," she laughed.

"Yes, it is, but I am sure we will warm up in the Jacuzzi, it should be ready in a minute," I said as I began to undress, "You are a beautiful woman, this time with you has been really refreshing, thank you."

"You are welcome and thank you for keeping me lifted after that idiot soon-to-be ex-husband of mine tried to ruin my weekend," she said as exhaled in frustration.

I walked up and took her in my arms, to give her a hug of reassurance. I leaned down and placed a soft kiss on her lips. She returned my kiss with a touch of her tongue, which turned into a fully heated embrace. She gave a slight moan after feeling my firming erection.

"That was nice, you sure you want to get into the Jacuzzi now…should we give it a few minutes?" I asked.

"No, let's get in now," she said as she led me to the bathroom.

The lavender candle was working; there was a nice aroma in the bathroom. Closing the door warmed the room; I hoped the water wouldn't be too hot; it would be embarrassing if I sit down, and it scalds my balls. I let her get in first and I slid in behind her; the water was exactly right…the good weekend continues.

She leaned back into my chest and let out a sigh of release. I could feel her body relax as though she felt safe and secure. I encircled my arms around her and held her for a while. My erection had gone down so this time was more about relaxing rather than sex.

I started massaging her shoulders, which allowed her to relax a little more; she closed her eyes and said, "Thank you, it's been a long time since I had a massage." I was in heaven.

"This is probably all you need is to just relax yourself, you know," I told her, trying my best to give her an award-winning massage, "Leave all that stress shit back in D.C."

She leaned forward so I could get her entire back, moaning with each stroke. I continued the massage for a little while longer until she stopped me.

"That felt wonderful, would you like me to give you one?" she asked, "It will be a little hard to do in here but I can return the favor once we get in the bed."

"No, thanks," I said as I smiled to her statement of 'once *we* get in the bed,' my relaxation has come from seeing you enjoy the massage, I am sure you can find some other things to do when we get in the bed."

"I am sure I can too," she said as she turned around and straddled me," however, we don't have to be limited by the bed. "

"Yeah, but we don't have protection in the Jacuzzi, I try to practice being safe as much as I can," I said.

"Wow that is impressive, but my straddling you is not about entering me, I just wanted to get more kisses, but if you are not comfortable, I understand. Please know that I practice safe sex as well."

"I totally understand," I was afraid that I had offended her so I pulled her to me and gave her a kiss, "I would never think that you didn't practice safe sex, please don't misunderstand me."

"No worries," she said floating from the kiss that I had just given her, she kissed me again.

We stayed in that position for a while. I thought that her legs were tired because she stood and stepped out of the Jacuzzi. She wrapped herself in a towel and walked out of the bathroom. I took that as my sign to follow, so I followed suit, hopped out grabbed a towel and met her at the bed.

The room was still a little chilly, so she got in under the cover.

"Sorry, I hate being cold, I had to get under the covers," she said with a cute laugh.

"I understand, I am sure that you are going to be hot in a few minutes," I said as I got under the covers as well."

"I certainly hope so," she said as she curled under me.

We began kissing and I slid my hand to her pussy, it was already flowing, so it was easy for me to slide two of my fingers inside her. I fingered her, getting her wetter. While fingering her, I took her breast into my mouth and sucked her nipples, biting the edge of it just a little with my teeth; they were larger than I thought…beautiful. She moaned in pleasure. Her sounds of enjoyment and grinding hips let me know that she was ready. I didn't want her to explode from my fingers, so I mounted her and entered into a sea of warmth and moisture. When I entered, I felt her body tense as she let out a scream of pleasure; letting me know that I had reached her spot.

For a heated five or ten minutes, we were grinding and giving each other pleasure that it appeared neither one of us had experienced in a while. I was pleased by her flexibility as she locked her legs around my waist as I dove deep inside her.

"I won't last much longer if you keep doing that," I said between short breaths of pleasure, "I don't want you to think I am quick on the draw."

"It's okay, you can be quick because I am almost there!" she moaned, "The second time can be longer, just give it to me now."

With that I plunged deeper inside her and enjoyed every stroke as we both reached our climax.

As our bodies limbered from our release, I almost wanted to applaud, baby had skills.

"That was good, thank you," she said as she kissed my lips, and cheeks.

"Yes it was, thank you for not making me hold it, it's been a minute," I said as I laughed.

"It's been a while for me too, we have a lot to catch up on so take a break and get ready for the next round," she said as she mounted me and began kissing my neck, and slowly began descending my body.

My body was receptive to her movements; round two was not going to be too far away.

We went on for the rest of the night and most of the next day; the only hiking we did was on each other's bodies.

Later that afternoon we took a break to order lunch from the restaurant and shower. Patria took her shower first, I got up to get the remote for the TV and noticed Patria's purse and stuff on the floor. I picked it all up and put it on the dresser for her. Then something caught my attention. On Patria's key chain was a photo of her and her husband Jarell, the guy who was taking out the trash the other night.

*Damn, isn't that a coincidence?* I laughed to myself, they are going to be perfect for each other, as Patria and I will be too.

When Patria got out of the shower, I held up the key chain and told her that he was the guy who was in the house. She burst out laughing.

"From what you told me of your ex-wife, they are going to be perfect for each other," she said.

I laughed and said, "That is the same thing I thought, best of wishes to them both, and thank you because his loss has become my gain."

"Ditto," Patria said, a wonderful gain it is."

The rest of the weekend went well, Patria and I became intimate friends as we got each other through our divorces; supporting each other as we transitioned to our new lives. We did not date each other exclusively for the first year, sticking to our original agreement of not locking into a relationship. However, after the first year, we both realized that we were the best fit for each other.

Three years after both of our divorces, me and Patria got married. We are happy, living in the Fort Washington home I had built, with my daughter Talina, a one-year-old daughter, and a baby boy on the way. The romance novels that I write now are based on our beautiful, happy marriage. I never thought the second time around would be this great.

*Forever, For Always, For Love*

# *Time For Me*

I never thought the day would come when I would fall into the category of those who put everything and everybody before themselves.

I always thought that was the thing for those housewives that didn't have anything going for themselves. I always felt bad when I would here women saying they never shopped for themselves, always for the kids or the house and I would look at them and think, *"I can tel.,"*

I felt selfish because, while my daughters never lacked for anything, mama was never left out. Shop for them, shop for me was always my motto. But, as the old folks use to say, *"keep living and you will see a little of everything"* my day has come.

The economy has been bad over the past three years. I didn't feel it in the beginning, but now it has hit our home. I am a 36-year-old college graduate with eighteen plus years' experience as a Marketing Research Analyst, yet here I am holding a job as a Financial Aid Advisor making $33,000 a year when my skills and qualifications should be at a $70,000 a year job at the minimum.

While I can blame the economy, the bulk of it is my fault, underestimating my skills behind the comments of equally unskilled management who were intimidated by the potential they saw in me…that I did not see in myself.

My girlfriend TJ and I laugh at our situations because we both enjoy doing jobs that seem to get cut first when a company is downsizing.

TJ's love is Marketing and Event planning. While the bulk of my career has been in research, I became interested in it as well and was extremely good at it for someone who did not have formal training. Our joke is that when times get hard in a company, they stop researching, marketing and planning.

Ironically TJ and I now work in the same industry. She is an International Admissions representative at my sister-school. The owners of both of our schools are Education Careers Corporation, which owns over seventy-eight proprietary schools throughout the US and a few overseas. EEC didn't become the largest by a whim, they have worked for their success and believe me, and they make you work as well. TJ and I constantly email and call each other to offer support and trade horror stories about the students we meet daily.

If you are not familiar with a Proprietary School and its students, just take a look at the commercials for the schools advertised during Jerry Springer, Maury Povich, or any of the judge shows. These advertisements promote establishing or changing careers by attending their school for seven to nine months and getting a certificate as a Medical Assistant, Accounting Clerk or fifty other jobs and that is a Proprietary School. If you pay attention to the audiences of these shows you will see the general makeup of students that attend the schools.

I have never worked a job that has made me feel like I have no time for anything; I feel like I am there every hour of the day, and it is exhausting. By the time I go to work, come home to my husband and ten-year-old twin daughters, I don't have any time for myself.

It is very draining, and I am starting to look like it. I have picked up a few pounds and my face looks tired. This is even more depressing because I was once an energized aerobics instructor for six years and I gave it up because of the hours on this job!

TJ has been harassing me to take time out and spend the day in the spa with our other girlfriends, V, Mary and Shandle. They have been waiting for me to take the time to go, but now the pressure is on, and they are going without me.

At first, I was indignant, and told them to go ahead, because I really don't have the money and a good day's sleep is all I needed anyway. But after this last week at work, preparing for our annual accreditation visit, I was the first one running to the door of Spa Sharece.

Spa Sharece is African American owned business located in the West End area of Atlanta, Georgia, and is a part of the City's move toward neighborhood revitalization. The West End sits at the backside of Morehouse college and was once a very nice area. It has seen some tough times in the recent years but is back on the upswing.

Spa Sharece has been open now for a year and has gotten rave reviews since day one. They offer full body massages, facials, manicures, pedicures and body waxes. The wonderful thing about them is that they use all natural products developed by the owners. I can't tell you how many times I have heard women scream about how wonderful the place is.

The appointments stretch out over a year; more of a reason for me to drop everything for this appointment, because we were able to get in within a week.

TJ called to book an appointment and the closet thing they had was three months away. Just so happen one of her co-workers who frequents often with three of her cousins had death in the family, so they would not be able to keep their appointment.

When we get to the spa it is everything that I have heard it to be. It is like walking into the Arabian Palaces I would see in black and white TV movies when I was a little girl; only this was in color.

When you walked in, you felt as though someone was wrapping their arms around you. There was an aroma of Rosemary and Lavender that just relaxed you with every breath. When you first walk in, you remove your shoes while they check you in. We then went to the waiting room until our group escort arrived. I don't know about the ladies, but I could have just stayed right there in the waiting room and been happy.

There was a large brick-framed fireplace in the center of the room; plush wine- and cream-colored chairs circled the room giving everyone equal exposure to the fire. The chairs were soft and made of a velour material. I swear it felt like someone had wrapped me in blanket like a baby. Each chair had an ottoman made of the same material as the chair. They served us Champagne with Chocolate Strawberries. It was an awesome experience.

Our valet came in after about fifteen minutes and took us to the dressing room where we showered and slipped into beautiful wine and cream plush robes and matching slippers which matched the chairs that were in the lounge area.

Although we came as a group, the Spa emphasizes individual treatment and encourages each person to enjoy their time privately. So, I decided to start with a full body massage, TJ started with the manicure and pedicure, Shandle started with the facial and Mary and V chose the deep tissue cleanse.

After the Champagne and hot shower, I was pretty relaxed so I didn't feel that the masseuse was going to have too much to do. The guide escorted me up to the second floor and I could not believe what I saw. Standing at the door of room where I was getting my massage was the most beautiful Black man I have ever seen. He was 6'5" and about 230 pounds of muscle; not the I am so tight I can't move muscle, but the smooth soft eloquently defined muscle. He had milk chocolate caramel skin with bright dark eyes and I'll just be damned if the man didn't have the prettiest teeth I have ever seen and he had dimples.

How was I going to let this man touch me without creaming all over myself? The tension that I thought was gone had now consumed me once again. I immediately went into body check mode. Had I showered well? Did I shave under my arms? Did the carpet match the curtains? Oh my God did I shower well?

His name was Amarre, and he had a very sensual voice. What was this place trying to do to me? How could I lie on the table and let the man put his hands on my body and not roll over and throw my legs open and just tell him to take me?

He opened the door for me and as I was entering the room, he placed his hands in the bottom of my back to escort me in. His hands were huge and emanated a heat that went straight to my coochie!

Oh well it's over now, because I felt a twinge and I know released some fluid. I could only hope it was a little and immediately began to pray that I would not embarrass myself by attacking this man. I was relieved when I saw a box of Kleenex on the counter. Good, I would wipe myself when he steps out while I get on the table.

I had never disclosed this to my girls, but my love life at home has been lacking. The frequency and intensity is nothing like it used to be. A sista has not been getting served like she needs to and if Amarre is half as good sexually as he looks, I could set it off up in here today!

I was really proud of myself, because although this is what I was feeling on the inside, my outside demeanor was really calm…until I noticed what appeared to be a gleam of pleasure in his eyes when he told me to remove my robe, lie face down on the table and place the towel over me, and he didn't make any attempt to turn around or leave the room.

I stood there and looked into those gorgeous eyes in protest until he reluctantly left the room after popping in the Jazz CD.

I then removed my robe, quickly wiped myself with the Kleenex laid on the table and threw the blanket over me. He asked me if I had a preference of beginning at the head or feet; fighting the temptation to throw my legs open and *say right here please right here*, I told him the feet would be great.

He smiled as if he could read my true thoughts and walked to the end of the table to begin. He gently lifted my right foot and began to massage in the center then moved to my toes. He continued this motion as I lay with my face in the circular stirrup; I closed my eyes and began to visualize his movements. I could feel the tension easing out of my body as I slipped into a feeling of complete tranquility. His movements were so swift and soft as he worked magic on my feet; a few times it felt as though he was sucking my toes! I laughed to myself as I realized that the Champagne was really taking full effect.

As he left my feet, I began to feel his warm hands run up and down my legs as he worked to increase the blood circulation. The one thing that I maintain is my love for running. I used to average twenty miles per week, but I only get in about ten now; as a result, my legs were very tight, so his hands were a welcome relief.

He placed my right foot in the center chest and used his thumbs to gently massage the tension knots out of my legs. I let out a sensual moan as I enjoyed the feeling of his hands on my legs, the slight breeze that caressed my clitoris as he lifted my leg and the warmth of his chest on my feet. I felt his chest flex as he laughed at my moans…I think he was pleased that I was showing signs of pleasure from his work. He repeated these movements on my left leg, which gave me a repeat of the sensual feelings and I continued to moan…I was in heaven.

When he finished with the left leg he placed it back on the table, leaving them slightly open as he began to work on my thighs; he was leaving room for his hands to circulate the entire thigh.

I was so embarrassed because it seemed with every stroke, he made on my thighs my girl twitched. I could only pray that I wasn't generating any juices and if I were that they would not begin to flow. I began to make conversation to take my mind away from the sensation of his touch.

"You are really good, how long have you been a masseuse?" I asked.

"I have been doing this for about 15 years and I love every minute of it. There is nothing like hearing the pleasures that my touch can bring," he said seductively.

Well damn! Just when I was trying to move away from heated thoughts, his response only heated me more. I might as well pray now for the sin I know I will be committing.

I let out a small giggle at my thought…there is no way this man would risk his career by attempting to have sex; I know the champagne is making me delusional.

Just as I was attempting to convince myself that what I thought was happening was a fantasy, his hands began to move up my thigh and it seemed that his breathing was getting heavy. Still trying to deny what was becoming obvious, I dismissed the breathing as him being exasperated from the massage. I had heard somewhere that giving massages can really drain your energy…yeah right.

As he moved up my thigh my body tensed a little because his hands were getting closer to my garden, which, by now was moist with anticipation. I started to hop off the table and run out of the room because I knew that if I allowed him to continue the only thing left to do was roll over on my back and wrap my legs around his neck!

I began to say a silent prayer instead; this was a professional establishment so it had to be my imagination, surely this man would not be intentionally trying to arouse me.

He moved to the opposite side of the table to continue the movements on my other thigh, it was more of the same, so I intensified my prayer of strength. This time as he worked my inner thigh, his finger grazed my lips. My body tensed as I grabbed the massage table and arched my back. I thank God for being raised well, because I was really at a point and rolling over and saying eat me please place those luscious lips on me and eat me.

The pleasure of his touch made my body relax and my legs opened wider as a welcoming sign.

He began massaging my butt cheeks as he added more intensified strokes to my vagina, which turned my garden into a rain forest. He knew what he was doing because he stroked just enough to please, avoiding bringing me to a full climax; I had not experienced this much pleasure in a while.

Realizing that I was not sure that I was ready for what may possibly come next, I reached behind me to move his hand away. I was about to sit up, but he gently pushed me back down on the table.

"I'm sorry, I thought from your reaction to my first touch that you wanted more," Amarre said with a sound of concern.

"I don't know if I can or should be doing this," I replied. "Please don't worry I am fully conscious of my initial response; I think I am just having second thoughts."

"That's understandable but please let me finish your shoulders, you deserve the full service," he said convincingly.

Thinking that we were on the same page and not feeling any harm from his actions, I relaxed and let him continue.

He pulled the sheet down to cover my legs and folded the top portion back to begin work on my back. The warmth of the oil felt nice as he started on my neck and moved down in a smooth motion to my shoulders. He did this repeatedly before he began concentrating on my right then left shoulder. He then moved to my back.

It was at this point that I began to let out little sighs. His hands were so strong, yet so tender. The oil was warm and was a mixture of the Lavender I smelled earlier and Eucalyptus.

Hearing my sighs he began to ask me if it felt okay and I could only respond with more sighs. I could feel him putting his entire body in every stroke of my back. He began to use his arms in a rolling pin motion up and down my back and my sighs

intensified to a soft moan.

With the towel now covering just my butt, he began to lift the towel to work in

that area in which I immediately tensed up.

"Just relax," he said softly.

"If this is an awkward area, I can keep it covered,"

I was not going to be a fool and say yes, I just said it was okay at which time I

could have sworn I heard him let out a grunt of pleasure. Not bragging, but it is my best

asset.

After he finished with my back, he asked me to rollover on my back so he could

finish the massage with a temple rub. Finish the massage? Oh no it can't be over already!

As I sat up to roll over, I realized that I was not the only one enjoying my

massage. What they say is true! What they say is true! His big hands meant that other

parts were big too! Oh, my Lord my Lord!

Amarre had an erection that was begging for attention. I was in shock and

couldn't move, but soon realized that my fantasy was about to become a well-awaited

reality. I quickly said a total of five Father forgive me's and protect me from all harm, I

reached out and slid his pants to his knees. There in my face was the most beautiful penis

I had ever seen. It was dark, long, hard and waiting for attention. The veins reminded me

of the embroidered stitching on my Patricia Nash purse, each we prominent and looked as

though they were throbbing.

While Amarre rubbed my scalp, I began to lightly stroke him up and down. His hands moved down my back, over my butt and into to my most awaiting area, which by now was hot and very wet.

He moaned as he felt my juices and intensified his stroke making me produce more. Of course, this left me no choice but to take him in my mouth and suck him as he penetrated me from behind with his fingers.

Both of our hips moved in tune to our sucking and licking and our breathing became heavier as we both brought pleasure to each other. After what seemed an eternity of fingering and sucking, he mounted me and placed himself deep inside me. Our movements were slow yet powerful with every stroke. We were in a rhythm, my body meeting his thrusts. Our lips caressed each other's necks, ears and lips.

The closer we came to our point of climax the rhythm slowed and deepened rather than getting faster and hurried. Each thrust sent tingling waves throughout my entire body, until I felt his body tightened and tremble with pleasure as he held me and enjoyed his orgasm, causing my last and most explosive orgasm as well.

We laid there holding each other as we placed light sensual kisses along each other's neck and shoulder and whispered a soft thank you in our ears.

Knowing that our time had ended, he gently lifted himself off the table and picked me up in his arms and placed me gently on the floor. He helped me with my robe and walked me to the door. Before he opened it, he placed my face in my hands and kissed me and said, "Until next time…"

I don't remember anything about the other services that I received. My body felt so light after that episode that I don't even remember driving home. When I thought about it later, we all seemed to glide out of the Spa and to our cars; I wonder if their experiences were as good as mine.

We never discussed any details of our services, we all agreed that it would be bi-monthly ritual, which we stuck to. I always requested Amarre and no one ever questioned why I requested the same masseuse. I now put everything aside and take just a little time for me....


*Until next time...*